I0592428

My Wife Karen

Edward Bennie

Published by Edward Bennie, 2023.

5742 Mogari Street, Ratanda Ext 7, Heidelberg 1441, South Africa
My Wife Karen
ISBN 9780796114952
Published in South Africa
By Edward Bennie
Pages 1-
First published 2023
Publishing/Editing/Design/Illustrations: Edward Bennie
Acknowledgements
Amazon Kpd

Table of Contents

About the Author

Edward Bennie was born in Eldorado Park, Johannesburg, South Africa. He got his love for writing when his mother brought home old magazines and books and he never stopped putting his pen down. He has many other stories to tell and wants the world to know. He writers on his Facebook page called bennians.

Edward Bennie enjoys writing freely away from conventional and traditional writing. He enjoys giving characters life and uses freestyle in fonts and style.

Introduction

Life can hit you with surprises. Your perfect marriage and perfect home can be turned into a hell hole within the blink of an eye. Things that are staring you right in the face could be hiding in plain sight. You never know who and what can come for you, so be vigilant all the time.

Chapter 1
Help me Fred

It was a cold winter night and the dogs started barking loudly, like something in the air was disturbing them.I tried waking up my wife but she was fast asleep.

"Honey, Honey are you awake"?

"Huh "?

I looked through the curtain to see what was happening outside.

As I look through the curtain to see what's happening outside.A bright light starts coming towards me.My wife still fast asleep.As the light approaches my dog became very quiet and started seeking for shelter.This light is approaching me faster coming from 10 meters away towards my window and it's becoming blinding to the eye.

"Honey, Honey wake up", I whisper to my wife but she only tosses over and looks away with her back facing me. The light came direct towards me blinding me and knocking me off my feet.Suddenly it was gone.The next day I told my wife what happened and she only looked at me and smiled.She had this thing of never taking me seriously because I tend to be playful sometimes, but I never lie.And even when she finds out about any matter I shared with her and the fact that I didn't joke as she still act with a don't care attitude.

Sometimes it feels like when I tell her something,she already knows about it and I am just boring her with details."What can cause this light, and where's it from I ask myself"

At work the dwindling thought of that light keeps crawling around my mind.I stare into the dishes and I my mind gets filled with confusion and frustration for not being able to get answers.I look down at my coffee that's turned into it ice on my desk and decide *to start punching away on my computer trying to find answers.Ufo sites, Strange Sightings pages and Light, but nothing. After work I decided to see a friend to see if he can explain this to me. Fred and I go back 30 odd years and have always been into Aliens and Supernatural worlds.He is excellent at what he does, but sometimes I think he over exaggerates and even makes up things.He is actually a Teacher by trade and in his free time messes around with ghosts and aliens. I always ask myself what he says to his students in class.*

I picture him standing in his history class speaking about World war 2 and suddenly switches into UFO mode.

"And yes class the German Army were super aliens who came to take over the world, but then they met with a strong Russian army of Androids created by Russia to fight the Alien invasion using advanced technology."

Fred is a great freaky man but funny.

I arrive at Fred's place and ring the doorbell."Come in" a voice calls from inside.I step into reading living room to find books and tools all over the place.I wonder what his wife says or maybe she's used to this by now."In the garage"he shouts.I find him busy dusting off a heap of old books and as dusty as his garage is,it looks like he's just taking dust from one place and moving it to all another in this dust bank.

"What's juicing man",as he likes to greet.My reply to him was" No juice at all"

"Fred I don't sleep at night and ponder the whole day". There's a strange light that I saw a few nights ago.It appears from a distance, comes directly from my bedroom window into my house and disappears. I need you to come check it out".

He looks at me from underneath his dust mask and safety glasses and replies with some playfulness in his voice,"sure it's not your neighbor pointing a bright light into your house to disturb your peace.You know the one that's always gauging your wife"?

"Stop your nonsense Fred, are you in or not"?

Fred fumbled and stumbled around his dust mask garage, stacking up books and tools while mumbling "No not this'' and handing others over to me.I looked at him and curiously asked.''Hey bud are we taking all this''?. With an irritated look in his eyes as to say,"Can't you see I am busy", he responded offwhat with a "yes,yes'' while lifting up his left hand as if to say" now shut up".

We packed all the stuff into both of our cars.Yes that's how much stuff we had.I looked down at the box on my passenger seat and there was this book with a black and white cover written,"Ghosts Hunters: A Guide For Dummies"

So my question is can a Dummy catch a ghost.I will have to ask Fred.

We arrived at my house and off-loaded all the stuff.I picked up the black and white book and asked Fred,"what's this for"?.He looked at me as if to say,"can't you see it's a book" and relentlessly answered,"it teaches newbies how to trap ghosts and spirits. Now I became more curious."Now tell me Fred,do you need hands on experience and come face to face with ghosts or spirits in order to pass your training.He looked at me and said

"yeah, something like that". Going through my mind now was, how can a person with no experience trap spirits because he has a book that says so.I think I chose the wrong man for the job".

We sat up every in my garage and we planned for the night.Fred spend 3 weeks at my house and nothing happened and he went back home.Until last night.It was worse and it's as if they or it whatever it is that's doing this waited for Fred to know leave to punish more.This time the lights came with sounds like a musical theatrical.Only scary and less jovial.Same strange thing happened.My wife slept through it all and didn't even bother to wake up even when I screamed like a girl." Yes you can laugh it's funny".She just tossed over and slept.

I called Fred and he didn't answer his phone but the next morning he was there 6:30 and anxious to hear about my experience the night before.Biting on his lower lip as he does when he is nervous, while sipping on his coffee in between."So tell me, your wife never even tried to take a look or listen to you and you say it's not the first time she does that"?.

I took a sip of my tea and answered,"yes,she does and when I try to talk about it in the morning she just brushes me away". Fred is not one to go into

people's private life's but he asked me," what do you know about your wife"?

" I know she loves green apples.She can't sleep with the same sheets for more than 2 days". And before I could continue, Fred stopped me in my tracks.

"Whoah,whoah.Thats not what I asked.My question is what do you know about your wife's background. Like where she comes from or her family or her friends or something dammit"?

At that moment I realized that I am married to a stranger.We met through a mutual friend and kicked it off same time and I love and relationship was a match and 5 months of dating led to marriage.She told me that her parents passed away when she was 3 and she and her siblings don't get along and that's why we never had anyone from her side at our wedding and I never meant to ask or delve into her passed because I could see she didn't like the topic.Until today, until this moment when my old friend Fred planted a seed in my head.

" Who is this woman I am married to"?.

Fred and I decided to go and see Lisa who is my wife Karen's best friend and wife to my old school friend James Colby, Jimmy as we call him.I told Karen that I was going to the soccer game with Fred as an alibi.We got to Lisa's house and found her in the driveway wiping of a wet dog that she just bathed. ' 'Come in guys,Jimmy is out, he'll be back tomorrow, so I got the house all to myself but I am getting a visitor later".We sat down and Lisa looked at me and said,"Park you look stressed". My name is Bucket Brooks.Growing up I got teased a lot for my name and I loved Spiderman so I called myself Peter Parker and the name stuck.I am sure many forgot my real name. Lisa offered us something to *eat and I chose Whiskey. 9:39 in the morning.She placed the whole bottle in front of me and I poured a double.Fred had coffee.I told Lisa everything and she spoke and we listened.But everything she said told us nothing and I started pouring more whiskey over and over.Until I was completely drunk.*

Just like me and Fred. Lisa didn't know anything about her best friend. Lisa told us only.

We sat there listening to Lisa talk.She told us that my darling wife came from a town called Riverridge and went to Walt Rim University and studied Pathology and that's exactly what she does. Karen is a pathologist. Karen and Lisa work together at the Firthlink University as lecturers. Lisa says that Karen has a brother and a sister all older than her. The only issue is that Lisa has never met them and has never met anyone who is knows my wife not one person.Karens parents apparently lives in Africa and she never sees or speak to them.I kept pouring shot after shot the more Lisa spoke and Fred had to carry me through the door when we left.Left with nothing as possible proof of Karen's background.That night I lay up whole night thinking and I never heard a word my wife said when she came home and I didn't even realize she laid next to me when she came in the room. The mixture of alcohol and stress.

I woke up and found Karen in the kitchen the next morning cooking breakfast."How are you sleepyhead",she remarked.I just grabbed my head and moaned."Yea baby you came home drunk and Fred had to carry you to the bed.I see you and Fred had a real good time". She looked so beautiful, this stranger, this unknown person wearing my soccer jersey, cooking breakfast for me." Yea we had a great time, did Fred bring my car back"?. " Yes he came about 2 hours ago,but you slept like a baby even when he tried to wake you up, Oh my Pete you". Why is she ending her sentence with Pete you. " What do you mean Karen when you say ,Pete you"?.

" Honey I am not fighting,just that when Fred dropped you here last night you were so drunk that you almost mistook the wardrobe for the bathroom and I had to help you. And you called out names in your sleep and started screaming and I couldn't wake you up, almost as if in some trans.Do you remember your dream honey"?

I don't remember a single thing.What did I dream and why couldn't I wake up from this dream?

It's Sunday morning and after we had breakfast Karen asked me if I am going to church with her.I was very hungover but I relented and agreed to join her.We dressed and left our house.A very strange thing happened on our way to church.A dog appeared from out of nowhere and ran In Front of our car.He stopped and looked straight at Karen while she had her hands on the steering wheel.This dog just stood In Front of our idling vehicle and growled at my wife, while staring her square in the eyes.I just sat there speechless.Karen switched off the engine and got out and our neighborhood canine just ran away into the bushes.This dog became scared when my wife got out the car and she just came back and said, laughing,"I won't be intimidated by a mutt" I said nothing the whole way to church.I just kept stealing her from the corners of my eyes.The preacher spoke, people clapped and danced and sang and prayed and I just sat.I sat without emotions,I sat without movement and I sat with thoughts only playing tricks on my mind.I need to find answers soon or I will lose my mind.It was a very warm afternoon and me and Karen agreed to go fishing when we got home from church and we had a lot of fun.Nature has a way of just influencing your mood and the tranquility just made me feel at peace.We caught some fish and cooked it over a fire in our backyard and it was amazing.For some reason I was at peace and I enjoyed being with my wife and spending this wonderful time with her.After dinner we took a long bath together, listened to our favorite music,had some wine and made passionate love.Karen fell asleep in my arms and I just held her and looked at her so peaceful and beautiful and I told myself to stop these silly investigations and let it go.

Maybe Karen is keeping her life a secret for a very good reason and she might be waiting for the right time to tell me everything.Let me give her time and these lights and sounds that keep attacking me might just be the neighbors or someone pranking me."Yes",Fred installed all these spy cameras and sound equipment but we haven't recorded or picked up anything and it's almost two weeks now.I am just being silly."Stop it Pete",I told myself "You're just stressed out for nothing, Karen loves you she won't hurt you".

"Doof, doof,doof ".A hard knocking sound wakes me up.``Baby, honey,can you hear that "? Karen turned over and didn't even open her eyes.``Sleep, honey I don't hear anything".How is it that Karen can't hear this loud knocking noise?.The sound was coming from my garage.Slowly I reached out to the flashlight on the pedestal next to me and softly crept out of the sheets.Like a ninja in stealth mode I slowly made my way to the garage. I swung the door open like a S.W.A.T operative, swinging my golf club in all directions incase whatever is here comes at me.Using my flashlight I shone in every corner of the garage,but there was nothing and the sounds stopped.``What's going on here"? What I saw made my blood curdle.On the wall facing the garage door, right under my garage window was written in black bold letters.``CONFESS BROOKS, TELL THEM WHAT YOU DID".I froze in my steps and what I saw next made me even more terrified.All the cables and cameras Fred installed all got ripped out of the walls by the sockets and were piled up in a heap of scrap metal and wire.Like something or someone trampled and stomped on it and sending a message to me to see stop my search or to push me to search more.Either way it was very eerie and cold.I went to my bedroom to find my phone only to find my wife sitting on the dresser stool talking to herself in the mirror.Her eyes closed and her head tilting side to side like someone singing a lullaby to a baby.She kept repeating the same words over and over while laughing a creepy laugh in-between.``He will know,He will speak,He will,He will"I stood there without any plan or strategy on what to do next.Then she suddenly spoke to me.``Don't just stand there honey.Come in Pete come sit next to me".I got more terrified this time and just as I decided to run away Karen fainted and fell down from the stool.I ran towards my wife and picked her up.``Karen, Karen,honey wake up".She didn't respond and I called the ambulance, they arrived in 20 minutes.They found my wife still in her sleeping state but assured me that she was still alive but can't explain why she can't wake up.I got into the ambulance with my wife and called Fred.They took my wife into I.C.U and told me to wait outside.Fred and his wife found me in a state of confusion and fear.I couldn't even explain to them what happened I just kept repeating,"She just fainted Fredrick,she just fainted".Fred just put his arms around me and said."I am here buddy,I am here".

Fred and his wife waited with me at the hospital the whole night.The doctors and nurses kept running up and down telling me the same thing,"We will be with you soon Mr Brooks".It's like everytime they said that I could just punch someone in the face.5:30 In the morning they came to me and told me that Karen is fine she just woke up.The doctors told me that they tried everything and couldn't find what was wrong with her and when they gave up hope Karen just woke up like Count Dracula when he wakes from his coffin.We were allowed to see my wife and when we walked into her hospital room she was sitting up straight looking like someone who just woke up from a good night's rest. I put my arms around her and kissed her softly on her forehead.She smiled and said,"Babe how did I get here, please take me home".I got my wife discharged and we went home.Fred and his wife took off from work and spent the whole Monday with us.

Fred and I went down to the garage to do our investigations to how and what ripped out our equipment from the walls.We checked the footage to see if we can spot anything.The footage shows a light coming through the door and went dark again.Then a huge bang sound and cables and wiring started flying all over the place but nothing shows what's ripping them out.Then the light came back again and went back the way it came back. Fred turned and looked at me with a scared and strangely excited look on his face and said," Pete, this is what I am talking about".I looked at him and with confusion had to ask,"Fred are you really getting turned on by this creepy stuff."He smiled and said while rubbing his hands together as if trying to warm them up,"Pete my friend this is the stuff legends are made of and yes it gets me excited".

"So Fred what do you think this thing or light is". "Pete my old friend of our search is gonna get more intriguing and we might find something that we wished we never found.Pete this could be alien or it could be supernatural.It could even be a spirit trying to connect or send a message.It could be friendly or it could be a very dangerous dark force and we need to be prepared and get other assistance.But Pete don't say a word to anyone please buddy.I will make a few calls and get some experts on board".

Chapter 2
What's happening?

A week went by and nothing happened.In the meantime I have been doing a lot of digging into my wife's past.The only thing I found out is that her education is authentic and she studied for 5 years towards her degree.I also found out that she dated some guy named Phil Martin at her workplace and he resigned a month or so after me and Karen started dating.Phil's contact on record does not work anymore and nobody has any idea where he could be. I took a whole week off from work just to be concerned about this matter. My lovely wife continues on a daily basis with a smile on her face and a bounce in her step while I am living in hell.As if she knows what's happening to me and rejoices or she doesn't and doesn't see anything wrong with me.

The week went by so fast and Fred hasn't given me a call or visit since we last brought Karen from the hospital.The results from the hospital showed my wife was suffering from fatigue, but I would sound like a madman if I told them what I saw.So I decided to just put my fate in my buddy Fred, who for some reason just disappeared from the planet earth. My last day of break ends tomorrow which is a Friday and I have to see Fred.

Karen came home early and she found that I had already cooked dinner and she asked me to join her for a shower before we had dinner. We had a nice long shower and had dinner In Front of the TV cos her favorite show was on.I hated this show.Its about women shopping, eating and bragging about how much money their husbands make.Vanity on another level if you ask me.I just smiled at my wife as she asked me questions and made statements regarding the show and just nodded yes,yes, as if I could just throw my plate at the screen and destroy this TV for life. The phone rang as we sat In Front of the TV while my wife was tormenting with this program watching me die over and over.It was Fred on the line when I answered." Fredo, my chief what's cooking Bud" I could hear some measure of fear and hesitation in his voice."Are you ok Fred"? He paused and answered."Bucket you alone,If not answer with a short laughing" I laughed as requested and he spoke again."Pete please make sure you meet at our old school at the back of the old Oak tree we used to climb as kids within an hour brother". Fred only calls me Bucket when he is scared,worried or in trouble.This time I bet on worried.

I dropped the call and kept speaking as if Fred was still on the line,"Ok,ok, calm down buddy I will be there now" Karen got up and asked me what was wrong."Honey, that was Fred" she stopped me before I could speak." Yes I overheard and caught on,go see him it sounds serious.Don't worry Pete I will be ok,just go".

I grabbed my jacket and car keys and rushed out.I called Fred and told him I was on the way to our meeting spot.He didn't even take more than 15 minutes to reach me."Fred got out of his car and grabbed me by the hand and dragged me towards a dark shadow behind the tree."Buddy I hope you are ready to listen to what I am about to tell you"? I looked at Fred and felt my mouth filling up with saliva as I became nauseous instantly with the thought of what I am about to hear.

"Parker my friend, I did some digging and showed my expert friends the footage of the light we salvaged from the garage invasion.So the footage was studied and cross referenced with many other sightings similar to this.It was concluded that this is not a alien caused paranormally or even a human created anomaly.Pete this is supernatural and according to the experts,very angry and dangerous force of evil."I started shivering and it's not winter."What are you saying Fred.Are you saying there's an evil spirit in my home."?

"Yes Pete there's and evil force in your house and it's gonna come back stronger and angry every time it returns"."So tell me Fred how do we deal with this thing or whatever it is.And my wife,my wife Karen I left her at home alone Fred, what if this thing attacks her"? Fred lifted up his hands and rolled his eyes at me.It was dark but I could see him rolling his eyes."And this is where it gets interesting Pete. I did some research around your wife and why she never hears the noise at night or bother to wake up when you scream like a little girl.These could be the following reasons.Karen could be a retualists.She could be someone who has a family member that practices darkness or she could be a host, meaning she is hosting the spirit inside of her or assist it from externally.So either way she is connected". I started feeling more dizzy and nauseous."Wait, Wait are you telling me that my wife is connected to this thing and she could be the cause of everything.No I don't believe you and I can't think of my wife doing this.No Fred,no."

Fred stood there with his hands up in the air just shaking his head at me with disapproval."It's your funeral Pete you asked for my help and this is what I'm doing.But there's one favor I am gonna ask.Show no fear and don't tell her anything.Especially that you know about her connect to this thing.Act normal and get a Bible next to your bed stand.And lastly we must find your in-laws.Urgently Pete".

I got home and found Karen still sitting In Front of the TV.She moved over and offered me a seat next to her."How did it go honey,is Fred ok babe"? "Yes he is ok love,he just broke some expensive equipment that he borrowed from a friend and the guy want the equipment and not money.Fred told me that the only place they still have this equipment is in Russia and he is busy with student exams he can't let the kids down.So he asked me for advice"

Karen was looking at the TV and just saying yes, yes I think she's not even listening to me.

Friday morning,my last day of rest if that's what you wanna call it.My body just feels drained and I drag myself out of the bed.Karen is standing In Front of the mirror applying makeup.How beautiful my wife looks.She is dressed in a pinstripe suit with black buttons and she is wearing stiletto heels to match.Her hair is curly and long hanging up to her shoulders with s shining sheen look to it.I just sat there and looked at her with utmost awe to her beauty. She turned around and said"Do you like what you see?" And then she walked over and kissed me on my forehead and said"Morning love,I made you some breakfast.Its in the warmer.I am leaving now see you later and baby please remember to fetch the clothes from the cleaners".

I was dumbstruck at how beautiful *she looked and I just nodded steadily.*

The sound of Karen's car moving out of the driveway forced me to get dressed and contact Fred."Fredo".He just said "Pete I am going to call you back". I had my breakfast and went off to the cleaners.On my way out stopped at the Post Office to collect our mail.A big stack mostly looking like bills I didn't go through the pile I just dumped it on my front seat.I went got to the cleaners and found my old teacher collecting his clothes as well."Hi Brooks"."Mr Rogers,how are you sir".He looked very frail wearing a beige jacket and brown pants and brown shoes with a black shirt underneath and a fisherman's cap on his head.Mr Rogers was my 10th Grade History teacher and Fred was his favorite student.I think he inspired Fred to become a teacher."I am fine Brooks or so they still call you Spiderman". I laughed at his remark and said it's Peter Parker". He pulled up his cap away from his forehead, moved closer to me and said,"Same difference".He had these big brown eyes and they could intimidate a person when he started

you square in the eyes.

"Brooks, my boy walked me to my car". I grabbed his clothes from the counter and walked him to his car.A old Passat Station wagon.Gold in color with a oak beading on the side.Classic he calls it. ' 'Brooks my boy I passed by your house the other day and I didn't know it was your house until Fred told me yesterday.Brooks my boy do you know who the owners of that house was my boy? I mean the house you and your wife what's her name again.Ya Karen.The house that you and your wife stay in was owned by the Rocksher family.The father was a Judge in the high court and the mother was a University Lecturer just like your wife.They had 3 children.A boy,his name was Micheal and two daughters, Lora and

Emily the youngest.One day they just upped and left and nobody knows what the reasons was for this.I was surprised to see people live in that house it's been empty for years. Brooks my boy the Rocksher family was some type of Natives but they didn't show in their features cos they had mixed blood from the mothers side. The judge had his mother living with them and strangely enough my boy nobody ever laid an eye on her from close range. People said they heard from the maid that there was an old woman living there and even when visitors came she was always in her room.Some people said they would see her standing at the window from her bedroom on the top floor and she would stand there for hours without any movement.She never went on trips with the family and never went out of the house." I looked at Mr Rogers as he spoke and onething went through my mind. ' 'I have to find out more about the previous owners and who and what they were and what happened to them?" Mr Rogers packed his clothes in the back seat of his Passat and got in.I stood there looking at him with questions. ' 'Brooks, my boy came around my house for some tea and we can talk some more". Mr Rogers drove off and I walked back to my car.

It was about 14h00 and I heard a car stop In Front of my house.I looked through the window and saw Fred and two guys walk up to my door.Before the bell rang I was at the door already."Hey guys, Fred, come in come in".The two gentleman carried leather cases, sort of the kind that Lawyers use in court.They came in and sat down.The one was tall and dark with a big beard that covered his face like a balaclava.And strangely had a squeaky small voice for such a big man.The second was normal height with spectacles on and he looked like he could be an athlete.He was pale faced almost too light skinned was speckles on his face.And he spoke slow.Too slow for my liking.Fred introduced the tall man and Glen Burnie and the speckled man as Bruno North.They are experts in the field of dealing with paranormal activities.They have performed many exorcisms and are both ordained Pastors. They're also well advised in terms of dealing with interpretation and messaging from spirits and they know how to interact with the dead.I was feeling some relief and felt that this could give me answers I need.

Glen and Bruno took out equipment from their cases and started setting up. They put on their Priest colors and prayed before they started working and just as they started praying a huge bang sound came from my upstairs bedroom and we all ran up to see what's happening. We couldn't believe what we saw.My bed was split into 4 pieces and bed stand all broken into pieces too.On the mirror was written"BROOKS TELL THEM WHAT YOU DID".In blood.Blood that I don't know came from what or were.Bruno and Glen asked me what this means and I told them I have never done anything wrong in my life and it's not the first time I get this message.Glen looked at me and then at Fred and Bruno and said,"Brooks my friend we have a fight on our hands here and it's gonna become dangerous so I think you and your wife need to leave the house and allow us to work for a few days" I felt a strong presence of evil in this house and it's becoming stronger.I agreed to leave. I packed enough clothes for me and Karen and gave the house keys to Fred.I stuffed all our things into my car and drove off to my wife's workplace."What excuse am I gonna give Karen to why we have to leave our house for days or weeks on end and how am I gonna keep everything a secret to her?"Fred told me to keep everything a secret as Karen might be involved in this spirit hauntings."I hate sleeping in strange beds that's not mine"

I got to the University Karen works at and at the reception desk I requested they call her to the front for me.She was busy in a lecture and took 30 minutes to come through.My wife always looked amazing and even though these things were happening in my life,I was still madly in love with Karen.She walked over to me and kissed me.Her breath smelling of spearmint and her hair of shampoo and flowers as if she just came out of a bath."Hey sweetie,why are you here at my work.Are there problems at home or are you in trouble?" I looked at this vision of an angel standing In Front of me with her black locks shining so radiant.Her lips could not speak any harm and her hands could not hurt a soul.Karen was perfect.Perfectly, perfect just for me."I am ok babe,is there somewhere we can talk?" She led me through one of the empty training offices and closed the door behind us."Pete you're freaking me out, what's going on?" I prepared a lie and I hope it works. "Babe you remember I told you about the light that keeps coming into our home?" Karen paused and said,"Yes Pete I do get to the point". I swallowed some spit and said,"Ok we suspect that someone is playing a trick on me and wants to get me out of that house.Now Fred and I revised a plan to trap whomever is doing this.Fred got some friends to help him and asked that you and I lay low and disappear for a few days or so in order for them to work.

Karen was standing the whole time and decided to sit down. ''So Pete let me get this right we have to leave our home for your friends to play detective in my house and I have to sleep in hotels or motels until they're done?" I thought about what to say next and I need to make sure it comes out right. ''Babe do you remember anything from the time you went to the hospital?" Karen just shook her head. ''Now look at it this way the fact that you just fainted and don't remember a thing can form part of this strange lights and sounds coming into our home.As your husband It's my responsibility to protect you and this is exactly what I am doing now and I don't want to negotiate further"

Karen just nodded and said ,"Ok babe if you say so". I feel so bad.I feel like a liar and a cheat keeping secrets from my wife.But how do I tell her anything if I am not even sure who she is.

When we started dating Karen and I she used to tell me how her parents were never there for her and how her boyfriend cheated on her.We would sit for hours and I would just listen and comfort her.I made a promise to always be there for her and be honest and caring towards her.I became her refuge and her place of peace.I made sure that we never went to bed angry.And she agreed to do this same.We agreed that we would forgive each other through any situation and never let anything or anyone come between the two of us.Many nights we would sit outside and lay on a blanket while watching the stars.We would have a picnic by the lake and sit and talk for hours while we got lost in each other and our love was strong.Now we are keeping secrets and all the promises we made became just that, promises.We are lying and running behind each other's backs, who are these two people living in our home,because it's not me and Karen anymore but two strangers.How did we get to this or were we always these fake people, just that I never noticed.Just that I wanted to fill the void of the loss of my father and my mother and I just needed to be Loved and love too.I think Karen saw it and played on my feelings like a stringed guitar and how I danced to the symphonic tunes she played on my soul.Taking my every inner being and making it her personal playground.I thought I knew my wife,but now I don't even know her anymore.Who is this woman?Who am I?

15h00 The afternoon I waited for Karen at the exit gate of the University she works for.She came out and got into the car.On the way to the hotel she didn't say a word and was scared to say something wrong that could trigger a fight and mess up my plan.We got ourselves booked in and she went straight for a shower.

"Honey (she just kept quiet)."Karen".She hated when I called her that but strangely it's her name.I went to the bathroom and called her again. ''Babe,I am going downstairs to order dinner". Through the steam filled shower glass and waterfall off warm H²O flowing over her soaped nakedness.I only heard"Whatever Pete". I swallowed my spirit and just walked out.I got her roasted beef and vegetables her favorite and got myself a chicken curry.I also got us some wine and chocolate cake for dessert.

My wife enjoyed her food and wine but didn't say a single word to me the entire night.i didn't know what to say to her and kept the peace.I took a shower myself and when I got back to bed she was fast asleep or most probably faking it.Who knows.I looked at the bed and sheets that was very clean and white,but I still didn't feel comfortable sleeping in a bed that had many patrons.Maybe due to a psychological problem that I developed growing up.Something happened when I was about 9 years old.Growing up we were 5 friends and we did everything together.Our mothers worked for the governments Housing Development Department and dealt with land and district distribution matters.They all went to the same meetings and drank at the same cocktail bars after work and they were all single mothers.We as kids went to the same kindergarten school and middle and high school.We got dressed in the same clothes as our moms bought from the same shops.It was inevitable.We guys were meant to be friends not by to our choice but by our parents close relationship.Our group was ,Me,Fred, Johnny Barre,Ricky Barre and Frankie Dowde.Johnny and Ricky were twins and were redhead crazies.Frankie was the leader as he always had good ideas on almost anything and he was almost a genuine genius.Frankie won almost every award at school year in and out, from sports to academia.A sporty nerd is what we called him.

Our moms had this thing of going out every month end and they would hire a baby sister to look after the group.This happened like clockwork month on month. Now going back into history.My father was a police officer and he got killed during a heist gone wrong.He was at the wrong place at the wrong time.He got a call on his police radio that a robbery was in progress only 10 km from where he was.On that day my father was alone as his partner called in sick that day.My day found the perpetrators in that act and called for backup that took very long.A shootout started between him and the 4 criminals and my father shot and killed 2 and injured the other 2 getting injured himself in the process.Backup arrived and found my father bleeding from his injuries.The 2 injured criminals tried to get away but failed.They got arrested and things took a twist for the worst as my father's own partner was one of the perpetrators.My father succumbed to his injuries on his way to the hospital.The government gave my mother a medal and money but my dad was gone forever.The whole department that my father worked for went under scrutiny and many arrests were made due to corruption.

Fred's dad was a sports editor and sometimes appeared on TV.He was very well known.They called him"Mr 100"He knew almost anything about any sports and his predictions were always on point.Mr 100 got famous and rich and went for a younger wife leaving Fred and his mother all alone.He still appears in papers and television now and has married 3 more times after he divorced Fred's mom.They should call him Mr Wife.He changes wife's.Fred doesn't care about him and doesn't want any relationship with him.Fred's mom met Mr 100 when they were at highschool and he was a track and field athlete and she was just a bookworm preachers daughter.They got married a year after finishing highschool and Fred was born 3 years later while his dad was representing his region in sports as an athlete and Fred's mom a library assistant.Fred has 4 other siblings and they have great relationships as siblings, maybe due to the resentment they share for their father.

The twins never knew their father and their mother doesn't even want to speak about him.They got used to having an invisible father that never existed or has a name or family.They never speak about him and we got used to avoiding the father topic when around them.Their mother raised them very well and with a lot of love and they never showed that they don't even know their dad.But sometimes it did show,maybe I recognized the effects alone because they would become violent.But I didn't complain it was great having my own bodyguards to fight my battles for me.Even when people teased me about my name they would fight for me.

Frankie Dodwe was sort of the rich kid in the group.Frankie's grandfather was the mayor of our town and a very prominent business man in many circles.Frankie and his grandfather shared a close bond and Frankie was named after him.Franklin José Dowde II.Frankie's mother and her father had a fall out when she got pregnant while at University and never got to finish her degree in law.That broke his heart and created a resentment towards his daughter.She moved out of the house and got a job at the Housing Development Department as an intern when Frankie was born because she didn't want anything from her father.But as they say children brings family and people together or closer.Maybe not all the time but sometimes.When Frankie was born his grandfather did everything for him and even bought a house for Frankie's mom because he felt that his grandson could not grow up in a flat apartment.Even when Frankie's birth certificate was made he insisted that the names he chose be put on it.Frankie's grandfather and his mother got closer at his birth and he forgave his daughter.Now Frankie and his mom has a bad person in their lives.Frankie's dad is a hardcore criminal and goes in and out of prison.He wasn't always like this.He was.When Frankie was born his dad was working as an intern for Many and Bulls Law firm as an intern.He was working hard on becoming a good lawyer and was on the right track.

Until he lost patience and wanted to fast track his destiny.He started working with crime bosses and helped them launder money.He got caught and got disbarred and all his dreams flew through the window because of greed.Mayor Dowde never liked him even when Frankie's mom brought him home from a break from University.Mayor Dowde saw him through all his facades.Frankie's dad lives with them for a year or two after he came back from prison.But that didn't end well and he went back for drug trafficking and possession.There were claims of murder but the body or weapon was never found.

Back to my phobia for hotels or strangers beds.It all started when we were having sleep overs as usual.Our babysitter Mandy Hughes had her boyfriend Grant Mills over as usual when our parents left us in her care.She got paid for nothing because we didn't get food or anything from her.She and Grant would smoke and drink and watch TV and smooch the whole night and we ate and did what we wanted.We were invisible when Grant was around.This day we were at Frankie's house and went upstairs to play on his dad's old drums.Yes Frankie's dad could play a wicked beat on the drums.And Frankie was decent too on the drums. Mandy never shouted at us even when we made noise.She was real cool.I wonder where she is now.The only thing Mandy was disciplined on was our bedtime,21h00 exactly and non negotiable.The "Quartet" as we called our mothers would find us in bed when they came back and Mandy always cleaned after us."Damn why am I thinking so much about her now".

This day at Frankie's house Fred started with his ghost stories.He was always crazy obsessed with the dead and unknown.Fred sat up with the flashlight lighting up his face started talking and told us that he once overheard Mr Creddle at the bakery speak to Mr Rogers our old teacher.The conversation went as follows."Rogers, do you know that the house that the Dodwe girl lives in with her young son Frankie" Rogers replied."Yes I do Creddle". While packing his groceries Fred acted as if he wasn't listening but was busy taping everything by ear."Well Rogers that boy Frankie's father killed someone in that house in one of the upstairs bedrooms and cut the body in pieces and disposed of it.Mr Brenler at the cemetery saw him bury the body in a black bag but was afraid to say anything to the police for the fear of his life and his family."

Fred with the flashlight in his face as and he made this eerie voice and said "Pete what if the bed you're sleeping in is were Frankie's dad killed the person".I immediately got out and went downstairs to sit up with Mandy and from that day that thought never left my mind.When I see a bed either than my own.I ask myself who died in that bed.I can't sleep over or visit without taking my own sleeping bag.And even through that I ask who died in that house or room I have to sleep in and I stopped completely with visits to homes I have no history about. The following morning my wife found me sleeping on the floor and she didn't question me because she knew I had a phobia.She just coughed softly to alert me that she was awake.I rolled over and saw her go into the bathroom.I got up and folded my blankets."Good morning honey.Honey good morning". Karen just kept quiet and I knew she was upset.I went downstairs to get some hotel coffee which I know she hates.But under the circumstances we had no choice.I could only think

about Fred and his goons and how far they are.They haven't given me a
call.Should this be good or bad? I got the coffee and took some apple
juice together with some chocolate muffins.The juice is backup Incase
Karen doesn't want coffee.

When I got to the room she was already dressed in blue jeans, white
top and sneakers and packing stuff in her handbag.Make, cellphone,
wallet and things like that.``Babe I got us some breakfast" She gave me
one look and said" I am going to fetch my car at the University and
I will get some breakfast on the way.And don't wait up ,for me I am
going to see Lisa,I might be back late. I just kept my mouth shut for
the greater good of humanity. She left without a kiss or hug, nothing.I
grabbed my phone and called Fred.``There were strange noises on the
other side of the line.It sounded like someone dragging chalk across a
black board.A screeching noise.``Hey Pete what's juicing man?". "Fred
Karen just left now and she doesn't even talk to me.She is angry that
we have to sleep in hotels.So please guys get this thing done fast so
please."Fred made a huge sighing sound and said,"Pete this ain't gonna
happen bud we are dealing with something dangerous here and last
night that spirit was clearly calling your name.We recorded it last
night,but this morning the recordings were all wiped.Nobody knows
how?" I got a cold shiver running down my spine listening to Fred
speak.``And you know what happened to Glen.He wanted to go into
your bedroom to try and find some paranormal frequency and
something grabbed him by his waist.

Dragged him outside and locked the door."

"Pete I don't think you and Karen should come back now and I
am more afraid since I heard this thing calling your name and breaking
stuff.Perhaps angry because it couldn't find you here.This thing is
clearly after you Pete and we need to find out who and what and
why.Bruno and Glen are getting some connections to this spirit and
it will communicate with them.This is our best shot to find out who
this spirit is.But our presence has made it more angry Pete.So stay away

until it's safe we will keep you updated." Fred sounded very scared for the first time in my life. "Hey Fredo, Karen might try to come to the house,so be careful he doesn't find you guys there."Don't worry, I have made a back up plan. We have a pest control van parked outside and 3 guys outside pretending to work.I called in a favor from someone who owed me." I couldn't help but smile.Fred was such an amazing friend.More like as brother and what would I do without him in my life since the Blue Boys are all living and working far away.

Chapter 3
The Blue Boys

Let me introduce you the The Blue Boys.Growing up there were always groups and gangs with fancy names and dress codes.It was always something that every teenager wanted growing up,or perhaps most teenagers.We had Fred who was always obsessed with afterlife, ghouls, spirits and aliens.Fred had a library of UFO books and paranormal activities.He watched almost every horror movie and could tell you anything about the directors to actors.He knew everything about historical events and loved history.I understand why he loves history because it has a connection to all the subjects he is obsessed with.Sleep overs at Fred's house was very scary because he would make us watch his scary movies and read his books with scary illustrations. Fred was very good with math and science and history and won almost every award.

The only person that gave Fred fair competition was Frankie Dowde.

Frankie Dowde was a genius.And he and Fred was always busy with numbers and things and it was great to have two genius friends because we didn't need to attend extra classes,we had these two as our tutors.Frankie was very good at sports and really didn't want to become and academic.He just wanted to play sports and his Mom hated that.Fred always told him that he should have been Mr 100's son and they would end up arguing. Frankie was chosen as the leader of our gang because like his dad always had some type of scheme up his sleeves.I remember when we were about 12 years old we needed to enter a sing off competition and we had only one of obstacle.The Garner Kids.These guys played a mean guitar and they were the only guys that could beat us in the competition.Now the leader of the Garner Kids was Billy Hurt.And just like his surname he brought alot of hurt in our lives and Frankie hated him more than all of the Blue Boys.

Billy Hurt and stole Frankie's girlfriend Melissa Shikes and Frankie never forgave him for that.Billy was always a pain in our sides.Our first day at kindergarten he put a spider in Johnny's lunch bag and Johnny hates creepy insects.Strangely enough Billy and the twins are nextdoor neighbors but couldn't stand each other.Maybe because the rumors in the town says that Mr Hurt who is The Billy's father is the biological father to the twins.And if you look closely at the twins, they look like Billy.But the accusations has never been proven and the twin's mom always denied the allegations and stuck to her story.Than there was the time Billy took Fred's camera and threw it into the river and gave Fred two black eyes.I was next on his list.Billy stole my school bag and wrote vulgar words with a permanent marker in every single book I had.I couldn't go to school for 2 days until everything was replaced and I had to rewrite everything in all my books for those two days.Then came Ricky's turn.Ricky cried for days.Ricky was send to the shop for some milk.Billy and his goons found Ricky on his way back from the shop.They took the milk from Ricky, opened it, urinated into the milk and forced Ricky to drink.Ricky fetched his twin brother and they tracked Billy down and beat the hell out of him.Johnny broke two of Billy's front teeth and there was even police and social services involved.The matter was settled and Billy never bothered the twins again.

Now the competition was getting closer and we practiced and planned for the Garner Boys.Frankie had a plan.Frankie knew how much Billy liked Melissa and he had a plan.We got into the finals of the competition together with the Garner Boys, Pretty Girls and Hank and the Crew.We knew that we could win but the obstacle was the Garner Boys.So Frankie formulated a plan to hit Hurt were it hurts more.Excuse the pun.Billy would do anything for Melissa and I mean anything.Frankie knew that all the "It Girls" wanted to go to the new ice ring that will be opening same day as the sing off competition and the tickets lines will be long.Frankie heard Melissa and Billy arguing over this matter.Melissa wanted to go to the Ice Ring and Billy was performing on that day.The competition was earlier than the opening,but the only issue was the fact that the lines for tickets would be even longer after the competition.Frankie's grandfather was a partner in the business and gave Frankie VIP passes for him and 10 friends.The morning of the competition Frankie approached Melissa and offered her a ticket to the Ice Ring and she accepted with open arms.Frankie sweetened the deal and gave her 3 tickets to take friends.Billy got a message from his goons that Melissa won't be coming to see him perform and has already left for the Ice Ricky.Billy dumped his band and ran after his love.

The Garner Boys made a mockery of themselves because the leadman was gone and they fumbled through the songs.They made our victory so easy.That's one of the reasons Frankie is our leader.He is vicious and ruthless. The name Blue Boys was in our faces all the time.From kindergarten years the Quartet would dress us the same.Maybe it would be easy to identify us if we got lost.And within our group there is nobody that knows the other longer than the others.We met on the same day when the Quartet took us out for a mother and child play date.We spend the whole day at the park and we were all just 2 years old. We wanted to be cool and played around with crew and names for ourselves.BRFJF Inc, Smart Guys,Superboys and other names I don't want to mention.We went to the bookstore to get Fred some more alien books on a warm summer afternoon and as we passed the big glass windows of the house clothing store next door to the bookstore.Ricky asked us to pause In Front of the windows.He asked us"Guys what do you see".We all looked confused. I shook my head and so did all the `Guys can't you see we are dressed in blue.All of us and that's how we always dress mostly in blue colors.` I said,"Yes guys.We are the Blue Man." Everyone stopped me in disagreement and

Ricky said,"The Blue Boys". And the name stuck.From that day we became known as the Blue Boys.

At last we started winning over Billy and he started playing further away from the gang. 15 years later Frankie got married to Melissa and they have 3 boys now.

Frankie became a professional soccer coach and owns a Sports brand that supplies everything sports.Ricky is now a owner of 2 Restaurants.Johnny became a doctor and that was a taken for him.He loved nursing animals even stray dogs growing up.Fred has a degree in Civil Engineering and Archeology,but chose to become a teacher and I am Financial Advisor.We didn't do so bad after all.Fred has 2 kids.Johnny 1 and Ricky twins.I have nothing yet.The things we did as the Blue Boys are stuff of legends and some should not even be spoken about.Our college and university years were the worst,we got into all types of trouble and went through alot of joy and pain.I lost my high school sweetheart due to a drowning accident.Frankie lost his grandmother.The twins got framed for murder,but luckily evidence came out and their names got cleared.And Fred just got more wedding invitations from his dad Mr 100.At this moment with all these things happening in my life I need the boys.Fred has my back all the time and I love him to bits.But I sometimes feel that I put a lot of pressure on Fred.Even if he doesn't say it but I sometimes feel that way.

Growing up I was always the weak one in the group and the guys had to fight for me and stand up for me.Even now Fred is going through the same pain all alone because of me.Maybe I am just thinking the wrong way and Fred doesn't feel that way,but I keep thinking about it.The Blue Boys are the only brothers I ever had and know. It's time I assist Fred and his friends.I have to do something.What if something can happen to Fred?What about his wife and kids.And what are the Blue Boys gonna think.I need to start my own investigations.I have to and if it comes to it I need to get the Blue Boys on board if it becomes a mission alone.Soon

Chapter 4
Mr Rogers

I have absolutely no choice in this matter.Its either I need to work from home or take a prolonged leave from work.I called the office and let my manager know what my plan was regarding a leave and he agreed to me working from home.I had to many clients and absolute leave won't be very beneficial for both parties. I sat in the hotel room after Karen left and Fred told me what was happening at the house.I need to do something."Yes Mr Rogers",I was thinking out loud. Got dressed and took off to see Mr Rogers.I got to his house and knocked and rang the bell and called out to Mr Rogers but nothing.Just when I decided to leave the door swung open and big eyed man stood in front of me with a piece of chicken in his and chewing between words."Come in Brooks.Come in my boy"

I walked behind him and could hardly hear what he was saying behind all that chewing and mumbling."Sit,sit".Mr Rogers had a habit of always repeating his first words.If he started his sentence with, Hello he would say "Hello, hello." I sat down and he asked if I wanted anything to drink or eat.I asked for coffee.Mr Rogers had a reputation around the town for serving the best coffee.He was a connoisseur of fine coffee.He went into the kitchen and came back with a tray.My eyes surveyed the sitting area.I felt like I was back at Fred's house.The books were stacked, piles on piles.Others written,"Egypt and the Empires, History According to Me,The Origin of Men and many more.One that gave me a chuckle was written,"Do you know your Daddy". Yes Mr Rogers was just as strange as his prodigy Fred.I see why they can spend hours together.Birds of one feather.

The coffee was amazing and Mr Rogers didn't want to tell me how or where he buys it from."Ok,ok Brooks out with it.What brings you to my humble abode ?"He had another piece of chicken.This guy where does he get all this chicken he keeps shoving down his throat?"Mr Rogers,I need to talk to you regarding the Rocksher house". Mumbling in between the chicken chewing. I could pick up,"What do you wanna know?" He was dressed in silk navy pajamas with a matching gown and leather slippers. Like Al Capone in the morning.Only it was 13h00 in the afternoon already."I need to know everything about that house.Everything."

Mr Rogers sat down across from me on his leather recliner seat and licked on his chicken bone before talking.

"Well, well,where do I start.Brooks my family was one of the first members of this city together with the ,Rocksher,Dowde, Creddle and Hurt family.There were other families like the Boston,Negg and Colbert's.But the families that that was more influential in this town was Rocksher,Dowde and Hurt.We called them The Big 3.My father Mr Irvan Rogers was a brickmason and build almost every old building you see in town.And he made a good fortune as he became the number 1 contractor in the city.My father and Mr Basil Dowde the father of Mayor Franklin Dowde became good friends as Mr Dowde was our town Mayor at the time just like his son.Mr Dowde was the one overseeing all development plans and would send a lot of construction work towards my father.When Mr Dowde stepped down as Mayor he became business partners with my father.They started what you know today as Greer Civils used to be called D&R Construction.

Mr Dowde sold the company when my father passed away.Dowde felt that things won't be the same without my father,my mother got half the share."Mr Rogers got up and I could see tears in his eyes.``Some more coffee Brooks?" I could see him hiding his tears when he spoke about his parents.``Yes please Mr Rogers."

He came back with coffee and whiskey this time."Only coffee for me Mr Rogers." He didn't even bother about my comment and poured me whiskey anyway."So,so, where was I again my boy?I wanted to answer but before I could say a word he said."Yes my father and Mr

Dowde." Those two had a great relationship but they had fights too.But always managed to fix the issues they had.Good friends.Just like you and Fredrich.Good.Yes Brooks my boy the Hurt family always had doctors and pilots and engineers and stuff.They were academics.Mr Vincent"Big Vinny"Hurt was a pilot in the war and bragged about it all day.After the war he enrolled in University and studied some type of science and worked for the

Astronautical Science Department.He was a real braggart as you see all the Hurts are today. Mr Hurt put the town on the map as he was one of the astronauts to do a test run of a rocket ship before it went to the moon.News agencies came from all over to interview him about the rocket all sorts of questions.That gave him an even bigger ego.Hurt started what you see today.The Science Centre next to your old school.He made money as a actor later and started a car dealerships that grew to 100.

Franklin Dowde later became a partner in that dealership franchise."

"Now the history of this town has some dark secrets my boy.The Rocksher family.The family that you want to know about.Well Brooks my boy.That was one colorful family.The Rocksher family came from a history of miners.And by judging their wealth.Means wealthy miners.You can even look at the way the Rocksher mansion is build in comparison to the other houses it shows class and status and for an old house it still outshines many.Well the Rocksher family were some mixed blood natives from the countryside and very educated too.They helped fund the first Bank we had.They sponsored many events and they kept buying businesses.They had it all.

Mr Rocksher was a short stout man with long black hair that he would never cut.He chose to trim but not cut.His wife was a beautiful tall model,but not the lazy ones.A very smart and educated woman herself that came from money too.Mr Rocksher was the eldest amongst all the father's in the town.And he used it as his trump card at town meetings and he loved seeing the frustration on people's faces when he said,"Don't talk to me that way I am older than you."

Mr Rocksher and his family were very nice people and everyone loved them.Mr Rocksher had one secret or maybe two or more.He had a teenage daughter that didn't stay with him.She had a child out of wedlock and nobody knew her or how she looks.We all just heard from the people working in the household when they spoke.Mr Rocksher let his daughter stay with his older sister who had no children.His sister told people in the community she stayed in that both were her kids.The teenager daughter named Clare had a fall out with her aunt one day for bringing boys into the house.And late that night stole her son who was 3 at the time and ran to her father.Mr Thandai Rocksher woke up that night to find his daughter and grandson, who became Judge Rocksher, standing on his front porch in the rain.He got them in the house and his wife helped them dry up and get warm clothes and food.When Mr Thandai Rocksher asked his sister what happened Clare changed the story and said her aunt beat her and her child everyday out of frustration for not having a child of her own.Which to me was all lies.I met Thandai's sister, Yanda a few times and she was the most soft spoken person ever.Well long story short.Mr Rocksher took his grandson and daughter.But out of shame Clare never went out of the house.Mr Rocksher and his wife did everything for little Thomas as his mom just stayed in her room.She would stand by her bedroom window and just watch people go by."

"When Thomas started school his grandparents were there.When he got into law school his grandparents were there even when he brought home his first girlfriend.Clare never left her room.She even requested a bathroom be build in her room just to avoid others.When Thandai passed away she didn't even go to the funeral not even to her mother's funeral.But even On Thomas's wedding day she never went.But the amazing thing is that she raised all her grandchildren from within those walls and they loved her" I was amazed at all the things Mr Rogers was saying and I had to ask,"does Clare still live sir?"

"The last time they left she was still alive, my boy."

"Tell me Mr Rogers did Thomas ever find out who his father was?" While sipping on his whiskey he answered,"No he never did, it was a secret." Mr Brooks stood up again and brought back a photo album with pictures.

" Can you see Brooks,here is Mr Thandai Rocksher and his wife Helga and here is Evan Rocksher,Helga and Thandai's son and June and Clare their daughters.In this picture we have Thomas and his grandfather and on this picture is an adult Thomas with his wife Deena and their kids, Micheal,Lora and Emily."

I looked at the picture and there was something about them.Its as if I have seen them before but I can't remember where."

"Brooks the people working in the Rocksher household told stories of strange smells and chanting coming from Clare's room and even saw smoke and light.Her room was always dark even at night she even took out the lights.The staff believed she was some type of witch or sorcerer and they never tried to enter her room.A servant once tried to peek into her room when she forgot to close it properly.He just ran out and never came back ever again.He probably saw something he wasn't supposed to see."

This information was overwhelming and I had to get deeper into this. I need to find out what happened to the Rocksher family and why they suddenly left without a word."Mr Rogers,tell me sir.Who runs the Rocksher businesses around here and who is in charge of all their affairs?"

"Brooks my boy the person that assisted you to buy the Rocksher house is the person you should ask that question." Karen was the one dealing with everything from putting in a price to getting everything signed off.I was always busy and she would bring forms home for me to sign.I never saw the person I only saw his name on the paperwork and the money I paid into Karen's account and she did all transfers. The name was Zane Gold. I need to find this Gold person. Mr Rogers was getting drunk now and that was my que to leave. "Mr Rogers, sir I thank you for everything but I will be back if I need more answers."

Mr Rogers stopped me before I could leave and asked me. "Brooks, do you know that I once saw Clare in the garden at night when I came back from a friend. I had an obsession of passing that house because I wanted to see Clare from her window. She had a vase in her hand and looked like she was burying it in the garden. What you need to do is find that vase and we can find out what the contents was and its origin. Secondly my boy found out where the Rocksher family came from and went to. Go now, go."

Mr Rogers was drunk. I Left and called Karen to find out if she was ok. My wife sounded like she didn't want to talk to me. I could pick up with her , "uh and ah." At Least she was ok. Fred was on the line as soon as I dropped to call on Karen.

"Pete, Pete". His line was bad. "Fred, I can hear you, is everything ok?" He sounded very scared. "What's happening Fredo?"

"Man you won't believe what just happened. One of the pest control boys went downstairs to the basement to catch a smoke of weed and we found him chained to a chair and on his bare exposed chest was written, BRING BROOKS BACK. Hearing this made me feel weak to my knees and I almost fell down. A cold chill went down my spine. Whatever this thing is it wants me and it's clear now.

"Now what about the pest control guy?" Fred gave a soft sigh and said, "He is alive but very shaken. He keeps repeating. BRING BROOKS BACK, over and over and he goes into fits attacks and when he recovers he repeats the words over again. Glen called in a favor and they took him away to a safehouse owned by his church. They need to keep him there Incase the spirit wants to use him. The other guy quit and left immediately so we need to find another plan incase Karen comes around.

"Fred I also spoke to Mr Rogers and he gave me some background information about the town and the house I stay in.So I hope Glen and Bruno can cope alone. I need us to take a road trip my friend?" Fred agreed very fast I almost laughed ,my friend was really scared and needed a way out of that house without looking like a coward. I had to formulate an excuse for Karen and I don't know how.She can't stay in a hotel room while I am away and she can't go back home.I need to get Lisa on the case.But what if Lisa speaks the truth and let slip on everything.That could be a big problem."Think Pete,think man".Now I am thinking out loud again.Karen has a way of giving someone the third degree until you start singing like a canary.What if she gets Lisa to confess.And the lesser Lisa knows the better.I need to get assurance from Lisa that Karen never finds out about my visit with Fred and Jimmy has to know so he can keep Lisa under wraps.Yes I know,why didn't I think about this earlier.Our Marketing Director,Mr Winston Jones.

Me and Mr Jones has some skeletons in the closet.He has some kind of a colorful life outside the office.I once had a fallout with Karen and decided to leave the house for a day or two.I drove down to the Nickel Bobs resort and casino for some me time.Guess who I found there.Yes you guessed correctly.Mr Director Man himself.Winston Jones in the flesh and he was not alone.No sir Reed.He had his secretary on his belt and when I mean belt.They were practically glued to each others hips.Mr Jones had amazing winning streak on the casino's roulette table and through the winning and drinking, there was the celebratory smooching between him and secretary Sharon Kinnear.They were surely having some great times on the tables, until he lifted his eyes across the table and saw me looking at them.He tried tipping Sharon off that I was there,but she was so drunk and happy and stuffing chips into her bra.

Jones immediately cashes out after the the next spin and dragged Sharon off towards the cash out counters and I never saw them again for the evening, until the next morning at the canteen were we had breakfast.He asked to join me at my table and he and his female compadre begged me not to say anything to anyone.

Jones's wife came from money and is related to the Hurt family.And knowing the Hurt family.They might just put a lot of Hurt on him.``Another pun, yeah".I crossed my heart and promised to keep our little resort and casino secret.But in the back of my mind.I always told myself that one day I would cash in on my chips.Today is that day.I picked up my phone and called Jones. The phone didn't even ring long and on the other side of the line his scruffy voice came through.

"Brooks my man.How are you my chief."

"Not so great Mr Jones.""What's with the formalities Brooks ,call me Winston." I hesitated for a second and said.``Brooks I need a favor from you.I know you always send the marketing team on field trips for weeks, sometimes months.I need you to get me on one of those teams."

Jones interrupted before I could continue."But Brooks, you're an advisor not in marketing?"

"Yes Winston I know that give me a chance to explain my plan to you.You will get my manager Trevor to sign off on what I am about to tell you to do.I want you to put my name up as one of the members that will go on the road trip.But only I won't be on the road trip.Only my name.I will send you reports that you will submit only it will be adjusted by you to look authentic.These reports are only market related regarding how people love our company and how much knowledge they have regarding handling their finances.So these reports will contain real names Incase someone wants to talk to these people regarding my interviews with them.I won't be signing up people so there won't be much paperwork.Now when my name appears on your list Winston your team needs to know that I will work independently so I won't be around them,but our stats will be combined as one group.With my experience I believe they will be happy that I am gonna get them big bonuses year end regarding my research.So my manager must just sign off and allow me to be on that list and you will make it happen Jones.And look at it this way.If this goes well, this idea can work in the future and get us both promotions and big offices."

Jones was quiet on the other side and it was like I could hear him thinking.

"Brooks my man, this is a brilliant idea.Why didn't I think about long ago.It will make it much better for the marketing to understand the financial side and the financial team to get to understand more about the clients.This will expand our company exponentially. You're a genius Brooks."

Was this Jones guy listening to me or what?

"Jones,Jones, wait bro.Stop just there.Did you hear the part where I said my plan is fake for now.I need time away and I want my wife to think I am away with work.Thats why I want it to look official on paper incase Karen snoops around.The idea we will use don't get me wrong but only when I give the go ahead and if Directors ask and want to implement it.Just tell them it's my baby and we have to wait until I am back."

Jones gave out a big sigh of disappointment and I could hear in his,"Oookay Brooks".

He won't dare go against me cos I still have my Hurt card. Then he started laughing on the other side of the line.``What's so funny Winston?"

He giggled like a sick child molester."Spit it out Jones what's the deal?". "No deal Brooks,I am just thinking what a sly slicker you are.Brooks you have a lady friend that you wanna take somewhere secret.?" I almost cursed.

"Bro I need to go do some personal searching for something and some people from my past and I don't want my wife to know.She never liked me delving into my past life.So I ask this to be our secret Jones?" He stopped laughing and apologized. This Cheating Director got me to lie to him now because of being too nosey."Don't worry Brooks I got you on this.Get back soon so we can become fatcats in this company." Without a word I just dropped the call.This guy made me upset with his filthy accusations.I am matured enough to go around cheating on my wife.Cheating is for girls and boys wearing adult clothes.A 25 year old can be a man, while a 50 year old can be a boy.A 25 year old can be a family building wife, while a 50 year old can be a street running,hotel creeping girl.All comes down to your maturity levels.Jones was just a big old boy and I pray his wife never finds out.I won't tell because I know they will break all his bones and I can't take that on my card.

Jones promised that by the end of this Saturday he would have sent out emails and by Monday,my manager would have signed off.So I can start packing now and get my buddy Friedrich out of that house. I wonder if Karen is really coming back today and I am even afraid to call she might just shout at me. Rather stay cool and do what I need from my side because the longer I take.The more lives will be destroyed or even lost in the process. What happened at my house gives me the creepies and I am starting to fear for my life and my loved ones. In the hotel room I sat down and practiced my speech to Karen and I called Fred and gave him the full lowdown.Fred's wife was amazing Fred could tell her everything and anything and she would keep it all to herself as if she doesn't know a thing.She knew what was happening at my house and she knew that Fred was helping me and going away with me this time again.She always calls me and Fred brothers even the kids now me as their uncle Pete.I love that.Karen and I are also very close and share everything but this time I can't,I am not sure if she brought this thing into our home so I need to keep it on the hush.I love my wife and it hurts me to keep secrets away from her.And what if Fred and the guys are wrong and my wife is a victim.How will I face Karen again.And what if she is involved.How will I handle it? Somebody help me. I am going insane. Please do something or someone help me before I lose it.

Chapter 5
Road Trip : Tears

Saturday Karen never came back to the hotel but she send me a message saying she won't be back she's spending time with Lisa.I didn't stress that much about my wife not being next to me because I knew she was safe.I was very concerned about what I was about to discover on the journey we are about to embark on.I got instant heart palpitations fast and heavy.The universe needs to grant me all the strength to endure this challenge.Will I be able to find what I need and how long will it take.I can't keep lying or ducking and diving for too long.I need to see Mr Rogers before we go.Tomorrow morning first stop is the Roger's home.I got myself as bottle of wine and all pizza for dinner.I couldn't sleep and my mind was playing tricks on me.

Next morning I woke up with a half empty wine bottle and a pizza box on the floor next to me. I don't even know what time I fell asleep.I took a bath and sent Karen a message saying,"Babe they're sending me on a work road trip to assist the marketing team.I don't know how long I will be away, but I will keep you updated.We have to be on the road by Monday morning but I decided to leave today to get a head start.Also to get a place to rent for the time I am away.Honey I love you with all my heart and wish I could see you now,but I can't.If you come back before I leave town you can call me to meet,if not then know I am fine.I asked them at the hotel desk to give you keys to the room incase you still want to stay here or fetch your stuff. I paid for another day incase.Love you with all my heart and know that I am just a call away.Pete."

I packed my bags into the car and called Fred before I left the hotel parking lot."Fredo met me at the Rogers house." In a few minutes I parked at Mr Rogers house and I could hear him and Fred chatting inside.I rang the doorbell and Fred opened and told me Mr Rogers is making some coffee in the kitchen.Mr Rogers came back with the tray and greeted me."Brooks my boy, you know Fredrich and I are close and he told me everything.I know what's happening at your house and I think it's very dangerous.Just sell that place.Take your wife and leave my boy.This is not simple things Brooks.These are things that we see in movies.Run Brooks,run my boy."I looked at Mr Rogers and turned to Fred who was just looking into his coffee mug.

"Fred, Fredrich, is this your idea?" Fred kept quiet."Mr Rogers it's clear that Fred told you a lot and asked you to persuade me to change my mind about this mission.Well Mr Rogers let me tell you something.I will run away and what if this spirit finds me again.Will I keep running away.Will I live my life on the road, running all the time.And secondly this thing made me discover that I don't know anything about my wife and nobody in this town for that matter knows her.Not even her close friends.Now tell me how will I live have this darkness over me.How will I live knowing that I am sleeping with a stranger in my bed.If these things never happened I would've continued living a lie.Mr Rogers will all due respect sir I am doing this for me.Even if it kills me.I had a lot of time to think about it and this is my decision.It can become dangerous or heated but I am not backing out and if there's a reason for all this I need to find it." Mr Rogers nodded in agreement and Fred lifted his head and said."Pete you didn't see or hear what me and Glen and Bruno and the pest control guys saw.Bro I grew up watching horror movies,but now I'm in a real one.Smack in the middle and I have never been this scared Pete.I woke up screaming at my house last night and my wife sat up with me all night.I was even afraid to go back to sleep.Afraid that thing or things might come and get me while I am asleep.Pete I love you and you know and I can do anything for you.But this time I failed and I can't do it bro."

I turned to Mr Rogers and said,"Sir, I need you to lend me those pictures of the Rocksher family and I need the name of the town they came from?"

Mr Rogers got up to fetch his photo album and Fred just sat there looking into his coffee that was getting colder in his hands.For the first time in my life I saw Fred this shaken."Fredo it's cool my man.Dont worry I will be fine and I appreciate everything you do for me.Glen and Bruno are at my place and they will get a breakthrough.Don't beat yourself up please my guy?" Fred got up, gave me a hug and wanted to cry before I stopped him."Pete please be careful out there and I will check up on you daily." Mr Brooks came back with the photos and gave me a piece of paper with the name Levensdown Parish. Mr Rogers told me that it will be a difficult mission as the town is very small with a population of 20 000 people and they're close knit.The possibility that I could get any information would be very lucky. Communities like those protect each other and secrets.Mr Rogers told me to hope that there's someone that hates the Rocksher family that way I can get information. I looked at the pictures again and the thought came back again.I have seen these pictures somewhere but I don't know where.

I said my final goodbyes and left Fred and Mr Rogers.I could see Fred holding back the tears and I felt them too.I walked on straight to my car and didn't look back I got in and just drove off.My phone rang just as I left the Rogers house.It was Karen."Hey Pete, got your message, anyway drive safe and take care.See you when you get back."A big lump filled my throat and I kept my tears back."Okay Karen see you when I get back." The phone went dead.I stopped the car by the side of the road and just let the tears out.I cried for a few good minutes.I felt lost and alone with no idea what's waiting ahead of me.I wiped my face, started the engine and hit the concrete towards destiny.

Chapter 6
Road Trip: Night Owl

My journey was long and lonely and playing on the Radio was Kenny G keeping me sane.I stopped 50km outside the Parish at a filling station and got some coffee and snacks at the convention store while they filled my tank with gasoline.I got the map of out of the vehicle and laid it on my bonnet to look at the direction to take.The petrol serviceman came and handed me my keys and took the money for the gasoline."Are you looking for directions sir?".I turned to him and said."Yes I think I do.Are you from around here?".He smiled at me."No sir,I am from Levensdown Parish. I came here for work."Was this my lucky day or what?"I am on my way to the Parish as a matter of fact."

"You're in luck sir.Let me see your map.Can you see here sir.At this next off ramp you turn left.Drive straight until you find a Lodge on your right it's called The Night Owl.You turn into that dirt road on your left at The Night Owl.Go straight and don't turn anywhere.That dirt road takes you right into the Parish you will see a board at the end of the road with the names Levensdown Parish and a arrow pointing right and everything is simple from there." This was truly my lucky day.The serviceman looked at me and said."If you need a place to stay my uncle is the owner of The Night Owl or you can ask for the Blacks. They own a nice B&B in the Parish town.I took out some money and handed it to him."No sir,I can't take your money. I love helping people.Just drive safe.And here is my number if you have any problems or need anything.My name is Edmond Yeast."I took the piece of paper he scribbled his number on and he walked away and wished me luck in finding what I am looking for.I thanked him and got into my car.

I took the direction as he told me and got there in no time.It was dark now about 20h00 and the road was dark too.I reached the Owl and stopped on the side of the road across the Owl.I walked in.The place was warm think they had a furnace.The was that of roast beef and peach cider, with a blend of oakpine.Its was very clean with wooden floors and wooden ceilings.Many frames and pictures hung on the walls and the front desk had a old Windows Desktop and a gold telephone with a oak and gold stand,a beautiful piece.To the left was the bar and people sat around

enjoying their ales.And further down were tables and chairs and some patrons were eating,must be the dining area.A old gramophone was playing Tina Turner.While an elderly couple was getting their grooves back on the dance floor. There was also a pool table. On the side next to the gramophone.This place was very spacious.From the entrance door at the helpdesk the distance was about 50 meters side to side.A nice space for a party or wedding.The lady with gray and black hair smiled at me and asked.``How can I help you sir?" She looked alot like my wife.Just an older version of Karen.She couldn't stop noticing that I was staring at her.`Sir, didn't your mother tell you that staring is rude?" I apologized.``Sorry madam you look a lot like my wife.You won't believe just how strange that feels to me." I took out my wallet and showed her a picture of Karen.She looked at it once and said.``You got it wrong sir,we don't look anything alike." I put the picture back into my wallet and asked,"How much for a room madam?" She gave me a weird look and said,"No rooms available." I felt that I made a mistake showing Karen's picture.It made her upset but why.``Okay madam can I atleast get something to eat?" She became more aggravated and said,"Sir the food is finished and there's no rooms available and the beer here is not good enough for city people like you.So my advice is turn your shiny vehicle around and go back home Mr." I turned around without a word and got into my vehicle. And drove off towards the Parish.I was speeding off down the dirt road until I reached the Parish.I got to a small coffee shop on the entrance of the right side of the town.I stopped In Front of it,got out and went in."The few people sitting there looked at me weird and didn't reply even when I greeted them.The lady serving coffee at the shop came to me and asked,"Are you the city guy that spoke to Edmond.Edmond Yeast from the garage.`` She was wearing a baby blue apron with the words written in white on the chest."Cuppa Jack."That's the name written on the entrance door.Must be the name of the place.Who's Jack I asked myself?"Yes I am the city guy.Bucket Brooks.But my friends call me Pete.For Peter Parker." She laughed and said."Oh Spiderman." I smiled and responded,"Long story."

She introduced herself as Sandy Black.Ok she must be related to the people at the B&B."Are you perhaps related to the Blacks, that owns a B&B, Edmond told me about them?"Putting cash into her apron she took from the table she was clearing she said,"Edmond told me you're coming this way and yes they're my parents.I stay with them at the B&B.If you can wait few minutes until 21h00 we can go together?"I ordered coffee and waited for her.

Time went fast and the coffee was amazing, but not Mr Rogers quality but decent.It was 21h00 and Sandy asked me to help her carry some boxes to her car.She locked up and asked me to follow her from behind.This place wasn't as big as the city but it was awesome and clean.The view had green luscious fields in the background.There were 2 schools, Post office, Shops though small but there.A police station.Library and park and beautiful houses.Grass and trees neatly trimmed at every house and no garbage or litter and no ruckus.Tranquility in all it formalities.I could live in a place like this.

On the backdrop was the cemetery and nextdoor a beautiful big stone building with a cross at the top.Stained glass windows and a high roof with a bell.It was the church and next to it the Chapel.White as snow beautiful and if from an Italian painting.I sat there and just absorbed all this beauty.Sandy stopped in front of a three storey build with big windows all around.A big board on the sidewalk entrance said.Blacks B&B. She instructed me to park on the side in order not to block off other cars.I grabbed my bags from my car and followed her into the B&B.It was a nice place with shields and pictures on the walls, chandeliers hanging from the wooden ceiling and a big stone build fireplace in the corner with leather chairs spreaded around.There was a staircase next to the entrance door leading up and Sandy instructed me to follow her Sandy took me to a room right in the left side corner.There where 4 rooms on that floor and two bathrooms.I saw another staircase leading up the the third floor.I asked her pointing at t the staircase."More rooms upstairs?".She smiled and said,"4 more.One belonging to me and one for my parents and the other two only gets used when we have other patrons.We hardly ever have more than 4 rooms occupied at a time."I went into the room that was clean and smelling of potpourri and levander.Sheets were very white and there was a TV and radio and enough plug points.Nice.They even had a bar fridge and a wardrobe to hang clothes.A chair and a dresser, plus a couch in the corner next to the window.

"Welcome Mr Brooks.I hope you will enjoy your stay.My parents will be here soon to arrange payment with you and also give you the rules.But don't worry just formalities and they're softies." She went out and closed the door behind me. I was unpacking when someone knocked at the door.

Two figures were standing in front of me.The Blacks I said to myself.``Good evening Mr Brooks,I am James Black and this is my wife Pearl Black.I almost laughed at the name Pearl Black.Than I remembered my name's Bucket and I greeted them and welcomed them in."Please sit down Mr & Mrs Black." Mr Black stopped me and said.``Stop being so formal, call us Jack and Pearl."Then I remembered the Cuppa Jack.This must be him but I didn't ask.``Ok Brooks,the here's the list of the rates and roaster times for breakfast, lunch and dinner.You can choose to cater for yourself if you want and then you will only pay for the accommodation.Your choice." I took the list from Pearl and said,"Let me follow you guys down so I can make payment."Mr Black stopped me and said,"relax , finish your packing, you can come down in the morning, it's late now."I took out my sleeping back and laid it down on the floor.I got out the pictures Mr Rogers gave me and looked at them again.But still I couldn't remember where I saw them.Even now my mind was blank.I fell asleep on the floor and got woken up by a screaming noise.The noise came from the next room.I ran out to see what was happening.Mr Black and Sandy was there too.The lady in the next room was the one screaming.She was holding onto her nightgown and I could see she was really shaken.Mrs Black came down too and found us standing with the woman.``What's going on guy?'',she asked.Mr Black looked at his wife who was carrying a rifle and looked ready to shoot someone or something.``We want to find out too, Pearlie.'' The last started speaking and told us that she was asleep when suddenly she heard a scratching noise on her window.When she turned to look she saw a shadow coming through the window towards her.She screamed and switched on the bed stand light and the shadow disappeared.She was really scared.

Mr Black went into the the room and called ua all behind him.He pushed the curtains aside and said look it's only the big tree outside your window.When the light from the streets reflect on it.It creates a shadow and you might think it's a person.And the scratching noise is the branches swinging to and fro in the wind touching the windows.Mr Black even cackled as he laughed and said the same thing happened to Sandy when she was younger.Sandy just gave out a fake smile as if she disagreed with her father.The lady laughed and said,"I almost got a heart attack Mr Black." We left her as she went back into her room and we all disappeared into ours.Nothing happened again and the night was very peaceful.I slept well for a very long time.

Morning came and the smell of fresh pancakes tickled my nostrils.I got up went to to the bathroom to freshen up, got dressed and went downstairs.I found Sandy was gone already.I took out my wallet and handed Mrs Black the money and told her the money for catering is included as I won't have time to cook."Brooks my boy.Sit down and eat.Pur that money back in time pocket.We will sort that later.Money is not everything you know?"I sat down and thanked Mrs Black."Where's Sandy so early Mrs Black.And I don't see Mr Black too.?".She handed me the syrup and butter for my pancakes and said."Monday mornings Mr Black goes out for a jog around the lake and Sandy went to open Cuppa Jack.She is the owner there." I nodded my head and mumbled,"Okay, Okay",my mouth filled with delicious pancakes.

Just as I took another bite the lady from last night came into the dining area and sat down besides me.She looked well rested after her experience with the tree ghost last night.Not funny Pete I thought.She introduced herself as Maggie Sheppards.She also told me that she is a writer from Hillcrest and she came here looking for inspiration.Maybe even to find a story or two here.She told me that she is planning to be around for a bit of a time.``My name is Bucket Brooks, friends call me Pete.I am a Financial Advisor from Firthlink but I grew up 10 km outside Firthlink in Meyorfort.But I attended school in Firthlink and I know the town people as my own.``Maggie looked at my finger and said.``Married?" Is this lady a reporter or what?"Yes I am married." She sipped on her coffee and said,"Why do you look so familiar?" This lady must be a reporter.``I don't know Maggie.``

Then she said again,"Did you study at Walt Rim University?" Huh? "My wife went to Walt Rim as a matter of fact." Maggie smiled and asked "What's her name?" This lady is really nosy."Her name is Karen Brooks,her maiden name is Grover." Maggie got so excited and almost jumped on me."What a small world Brooks I know Karen Grover,we shared a room on campus and after University she just disappeared from the earth.I still have a picture of us together.Let me go fetch it in my room I will be back now, now." Damn what a small world this is.Maybe Maggie can be the missing link I needed.I am here to investigate the Rocksher family and I get a link to Karen.Two birds with one stone. Maggie came back and handed me the picture.Oh my word,it's really Karen just a younger Karen but it was her."Maggie is it possible I can make a copy of this picture?"

"No problem Brooks, you can just return it to me."

I couldn't believe my eyes and ears."Maggie, tell me, are you also from Riverridge like Karen?" She shook her head and said,"No she's not from Riverridge,I am from Riverridge and she is not from there. Karen never wanted to speak about where she came from and told me she doesn't see eye to eye with her family and her parents are in Africa." Who is this woman I married to.Her University is real,her name that her school friends know her with is Karen.But where she comes from and her family, nobody knows.

As we were chatting away Mr Black walked in sweaty as hell.But he looked good for his age.While stretching or maybe showing off he said,"Morning kids, slept well, hey Brooks tomorrow I am taking you jogging with me."This old man speaks and answers and questions at the same time so how do we answer.Maggie and I just nodded away.``Jack I keep telling you about your muddy shoes in the house."That's Mrs Black.Mr Black took off his running shoes and left them at the door and came over to the table, took a pancake off my plate and went upstairs whistling.``Keep smiling Brooks, keep smiling my boy." What an energetic old man Mr Black is?

Maggie got up from the table and said,"I am going out, Brooks wanna join me, check the town out a bit?" I got up and said,"Mrs Black, breakfast was awesome."We had pancakes,eggs, sausages and bacon.Mrs Black just pointed me to the door and said,"Go and experience the town,just go."I asked Maggie if we should use her car or mine and she agreed to take her car because it uses less petrol in case we have to travel a lot.It was a very warm day and the town was so peaceful.Kids carrying school bags walked on the sidewalk.Mother's pushing strollers and and dogs running around on the well cut lawns.A very beautiful town indeed.Maggie took out some bubble gum and offered me some.I declined as I hated Well tell me Brooks what brings you to Levensdown Parish.``I just looked through the window and said.``I need to find out about the previous owners of the house I own now in Firthlink.

Apparently the the previous owners came from this Parish and I am here to do some digging.Only problem Maggie is I don't know where to start and I don't want to step on the wrong toes and get into big trouble.I already had a strange encounter yesterday at the The Night Owl with the lady at the helpdesk I practically ran away from that place." Maggie looked at me and said.``Her name is Yanda Rocksher.She is the owner.Yanda is a very nice and soft spoken person.You must've done or said something wrong for her to act that way.``I took out Karen's picture from my wallet and showed it to Maggie.``I just showed Yanda this picture and she started acting weird and refused to give me a room or food.I just left fearing I might get attacked or something." Maggie looked at this picture and said.``Brooks, do you realize that Karen looks a lot like Yanda, how come I never noticed?"

"My same sentiments Maggie and when I said that Yanda got even weirder.By the way did you say her surname is Rocksher." Maggie nodded yes while chewing on her gum."So Maggie this means that she is related to the people that owned my house.So now that I know she doesn't like me it would be a bad idea to even try and get any information from her.Maggie can you help me.Maybe this is the story you're looking for?"

"Brooks this could be risky, why did she become weird and she might know that you sent me. It's not a good idea.We need to find someone else in this town that can help and know the family.We can even start at the library."

Things are starting to come together.We drove off to the Library.At Least I now know that I am on the right track to discover the history of the Rocksher family and all the answers to the ghoulish happenings in that house might lay in their past."Maggie, is there something else Karen told you about her hometown or her family." She just shook her head."Brooks, why do I get a feeling your wife is connect to this investigation.Cleary I can see you don't know a lot about her and she lied about many things from her past.Don't worry Brooks we will figure this out.I think this is gonna be my best trip ever." Man,I looked at Maggie and she was even smiling.I wish I could tell her the main reason that brought me here and wish to see what happens to that smile on her face.I wish she could see Fred and hear and see the things we did and still smile.Let me not mess up her fun.Yet.

We arrived at the Library and parked right across the entrance facing the gate.Maggie took out a camera and a notepad."What's with all this stuff now Maggie." She giggled."Research Brooks, research." The young lady at the helpdesk was very chirpy, somewhat like Maggie here."Hello guys,my name is Bridget Yeast and I am the Librarian here. Anything you need just ask me." This child must be at least 18 or 19 years old and in University or College not an old dusty library."Are you related to Edmond Yeast?",I asked."Yes sir, Eddie is my husband." I was confused.Husband at such a young age.But I didn't bother asking or delving deeper.The young Librarian turned to me and said,"Eddie told me you would be coming to our town.He called me and asked me to assist you in any way I can if I bump into you.Mr?"

"Bucket Brooks I said.Thats my name."As Maggie just stood there gauging this girl."Yes Eddie told me you were very nice to him sir.He will be back on Friday as he and his brother James take turns to work at their fathers of petrol station.One week in and one week out." She gave us a form to sign.It stated the rules and is written that we will be liable for any damages we cause in or on this premises or anything on this premises.We signed and she told us to go through the books we need or anything and just call if we need help.

The books were all shelved in alphabetical order from category to category.I was more interested in the articles and history of the town.I called Bridget over to assist."We need articles with pictures and history of this town."She pointed us to a huge shelf in the corner written.Levensdown Parish History.I looked at Maggie and said."With your big eyes you could see this information in front of us?"She shoved me with her hip and said,"Your's are bigger than mine." Bridget just laughed at us as she walked back to her desk.Books and pictures and newspaper articles were all stacked into the rack.We started sifting through the books and pages.Up and down we walked towards the rack and back.I even went to the coffee shop Cuppa Jack to get something to eat came back.Went again to the cafe cos Maggie wanted corn chips. We looked through all the stuff Maggie took pictures and notes.But nothing concrete.Its as if the secrets of this town are hidden at the cemetery.

Maggie took a lot of photos with her digital camera and wrote many notes down.``Brooks we need to develop all these pictures and search through them.I am sure we will find something that we have overlooked.These things need patience and time.I am sure there is something." I was just sitting there with no energy and words.Maggie amazed me at the energy levels and enthusiasm.She was just a super energized battery.Hopping and searching and cackling.When does this girl get tired? I finally got enough.``Maggie let's go.It's 15h00 already and we have been here at the Library the whole day.``She agreed and we packed up and left.Before we drove off Bridget came running and said guys here's my number if you need anything decided to pay Sandy a visit the coffee shop before going back to the B&B.Cuppa Jack was filled up with people today.Felt like they wanted to see the city folk.The eyes turned on us as we stepped into Cuppa Jack.Then an elderly couple came towards me and took my hands from both sides and led me to the other elderly people sitting at the corner table.There was at least 15 other people in the shop.All of them elderly.The elderly couple that took my hands stood presented me to the other elders and said.``Guys can you see we told you.Just look at this boy.``Maggie stood behind me dumbstruck as much as I.What's going on here?"

A elderly man walked up to me and introduced himself as my grandfather's brother Stephen Brooks.``Wait, sir , what do you mean by my grandfather's brother?" The old man took out a picture and showed it to me.``Can you see here is your great-grandfather Bucket Brooks,Me, and your grandfather William and Doug our younger brother.We were 3 brothers and I am the only one left.And here is your great grandmother Katie.My boy you look just like your grandfather William.``I looked at the picture and I really saw myself in my grandfather.My dad only had pictures of him at an older age.All my life I only had my mother when my father died and now I am touching hands with relatives in a place I never thought I would.My father never mentioned this place all his life.And my grandfather passed away before I was born and my father always promised to take me and my mother to his hometown but he never got to do that and he always called it with another name.He called it Peach Parish.I never bothered to check it up.

I looked at this old man with tears in his eyes.He grabbed me and held me very tight.I hugged him too."Great uncle.I never thought I would find my roots.I just bought a house.Things happened that sent me here, only to find my heritage.My father always called this place Peach Parish." Everyone laughed at me."We all call it that way. Haven't you seen the peach trees in almost every backyard.That's why we call it by that name.It made sense.One thing that made sense was my name Bucket.

Why didn't my father tell me that I was named after my great-grandfather.I felt that I should be proud of my name and show more respect to it instead of undermining it. Maggie came closer and hugged me from behind.I held my tears back.

Stephen Brooks asked Sandy to bring me over to his house because he wanted to get to know me better and to share more of my family history with me.My misfortune back in Firthlink has brought me new fortunes.Sandy offered me and Maggie a table and told us that the special for today was roast beef and vegetables.Karens favorite I thought to myself.Cuppa Jack was amazing.Its was a coffee shop and restaurant in one.Maybe because the town was small.But the people in the town hardly go to work.They have big homes drive expensive cars but they sit around all day how do they make money.I see few travelers come in and out through the town but that revenue is not enough to sustain a town?

I was hungry and ordered extra vegetables with my meal.In no time our food was on the table.My great uncle kept looking back at me and smiled.I could see some of my father in him too.The food was amazing and Maggie's conversation was good too.She was a very intelligent woman just like Karen.I felt free talking to this night screamer.Yes it's funny when I think about it now.A tree? Sandy was running up and down between tables and the girls helping her were busy cleaning and attending to tables.It was busy and old folks kept ordering more wine.I think it was for me.The prodigal son has returned.My great uncle invited me for a drink and I declined.I wasn't in a mood for alcohol, but he insisted and I gave in.I asked Maggie to join me and she didn't even hesitate.We danced and sang and drank and Cuppa Jack was was full of festivities.Sandy and her 4 staff members joined in.We danced and sang and drank until 22h00 at night and hour later than closing time for Sandy.Everyone went home at 22h30 when Sandy decided it was enough.Maggie and I waited on Sandy and and drove behind her back to the B&B.I was very drunk but very happy.

Mr Black was outside.Waiting for us.News flies fast in this town."Yes kids.I can see you children had a great time.Go to bed we have a big day tomorrow. Brooks and I." I couldn't stand up properly and Maggie helped me upstairs.Sandy walked up behind us and helped Maggie to get me into bed.I blacked out on the bed.Morning came fast and Mr Black was standing next to me.I slept with an unlocked door."Wake up Brooks let's go." Why should this old man torment me?Jack please I am really hung over. I don't think I will be able to do anything now please."Mr Black didn't listen to a word I said and just pulled the blankets down."Wake up boy I ain't going anywhere."I didn't have a chance with this old man."Okay, okay,Mr Black I am getting up.I took a short shower, put on jogging clothes and we took the road.Mrs Black was standing in the garden when we jogged out and shouted,"And breakfast boys?"Mr Black just waved and we were on the road. Past the Library, through the cemetery and down the old path that passes the winery,and left on a gravel path that led to the lake.What beautiful scenery.Mr Black and I ran 2 laps around the lake.It wasn't that big and before I knew it my hangover was cured and I was pulling ahead of Mr Black.He was encouraging me from the back and pushing me on.The fresh air and cool breeze opened up my lungs and I kept going. I felt renewed and wanted us to go another lap until the old bugger stopped me."Brooksie my boy.Lets sit somewhere and talk?"Why does Mr Black love to add ie to the end of peoples name? He does that to everyone Pearlie, Stevie,Thomie.I see it's his habit.We found a log and sat on it looking over the lake where I could see someone with a small boat on the water and wild ducks floating on the lake.Across the lake on the other side from were we sat I could see and old farm with many peach trees, but it looked desolated like nobody lives there.I didn't ask about it I was curious to hear Mr Black's story.

Chapter 7
Road Trip: Black History

Mr Black took a sip of his water and passed it to me.He put his hand and my shoulder and said."I think as a part of this town you need to know a few things regarding the Blacks.As we are part of the history.Brooks my boy your father Preston was my best friend and we did almost everything together.Preston always wanted to get away from this place as a child and we always spoke about leaving to the big city.Well I am sure you see a lot of people sitting around in this town hardly doing anything.Let me tell you why.My father Mr Aron Black.Your great grandfather Mr Bucket Brooks the one you're named after.And Mr Thandai Rocksher."I stopped Mr Black in his tracks and said,"Mr Black I own the Rocksher mansion in Firthlink now." He looked at me and said,"So I have gathered.Don't think we are disconnected from the outside world.I did some checks on you yesterday while you partied with your great uncle Stevie."In my mind I said it's Stephen not Stevie."Yea Brooks, my father and his 3 comrades used to be into farming.They worked on a potato farm about 100 km away from here called Hughes Heights. One-day as usual they plowed the land and something went wrong with the tractor your great grandfather Brooks was driving.He stopped in the middle of the field and started working on his tractor.My father and Mr Rocksher saw what was happening and came to assist their friend.Mr Brooks told Mr Rocksher to get on top of the tractor while my father check the engine and he went underneath to see if they start the engine what happens below because the sounds came from the bottom.The 3 managed to fix the tracktor.When Mr Brooks got up from the bottom of the tractor he spotted some shiny type of metallic object.He picked it up and my father shouted,"Brooks that's gold brother." I looked at Mr Black smiling when he spoke."What happened next changed their lives and the lives of the everyone in this town forever. The 3 friends spoke and planned how they would go about getting this to benefit them all. The owner of the farm was an old mean guy and telling him about gold on his farm would mean he chases them away with no jobs or futures and turn it into a mine or sell it to a mining company. So telling Mr Hughes the owner was an absolute no no. So Mr Rocksher being the smart one came up with a plan. These 3 guys were just 20 years old when this happened and they had no children or families yet. The plan was to get the town people in on this. Now the friends decided to keep the fact that they found gold a big secret, just until the timing is right. So the plan was to approach all the town people and tell them the plan they have is to purchase the farm from the mean owner and get all town people to become shareholders in this stake. Meaning every shareholder will get a percentage of how much they invest. And as production of potatoes grow so will their investments. The trio kept the gold part under wraps for fear of snitches amongst members."

"The town members agreed to this. The trio approached the owner with an offer and he asked for 30% more than what they had raised including the sale of the piece of gold they found on the farm. Mr Hughes wife always wanted to sell the farm and move to the city and she would nag him about it daily. The Hughes family had 4 kids and 5 grandchildren and all the children stayed in the cities and that's where Mrs Hughes wanted to be. She missed her family. The two of them had only dogs and and the maids and 15 workers and no family. The trio managed to raise the money by selling almost everything they owned and secured the purchase of the farm. That must have been a jovial day for Mrs Hughes and the Parish people too. Now Mr Brooks, Mr Rocksher and my father secured 20% shares, each as they raised most of the money. The towns people didn't worry much as they owned a farm now that will make them money. The trio decided to hire towns people to work on the farm as packers and other things and nobody else was allowed in the field or on a tractor besides them. The 3 friends made sure that all the gold they started getting out of the soil will be kept a secret and the money thereof will be used to buy machinery for the mine.It went well for a year and nobody in the town was the wiser as long as she got their profits monthly.Eventually the trio staged an act on the farm after a year and called all the workers to the land to show them what was in the soil. People went mad.Others even fainted and the mine was born.

They decided to call it Heights Mining Company.Mr Rocksher went to Law school,Mr Brooks became an Accountant and my father became a Financial Advisor just like you Brooks.Their skills enabled them to run the mine effectively and become wealthy and so empowering and bringing wealth to the whole town's people."Now you understand Brooks why they sit around and do nothing because the mine is still operating and we get our shares monthly."

My mother told me that it was an investment my great grandfather made years ago that's why we always had money and money always came in every month.But I can't understand why my father became a police officer and my mother worked for the government when we have all this money.My accountant is the one sending me monthly payments and I never thought of finding out how much my investments were .I just welcomed the big amounts I got and I only worked because I loved numbers and helping people.Not because I needed the money.But why didn't mom allow me to know I was actually wealthy.I think even more wealthy than the Dowde or Hurt family.Maybe my parents just wanted me to have a normal life and felt money would mess me up.Either way I need to see my lawyers and Accountant when I got back home.

"Mr Black got up and said let's stroll a bit. I want to show you something.We walked towards the winery and the smells coming from there were divine.Steam went up in the air from the factory pipes and Mr Black pointed towards the place and said that place divided us as people in this town and destroyed my relationship with my father and my best friend your father.I saw a tear coming to his eyes and I put my arm around his shoulders and he put his hand on top of mine.Brooks the day you walked into my B&B I saw your great-grandfather and your father in you.I knew who you were before you knew.Lets go have some food boy.Race you home." We chased each other back to the B&B and I didn't ask Mr Black any questions because I could see his spirits were down because of that wine factory. Mrs Black made omelets for breakfast, sausage and cheese muffins.I had everything on the menu.

"Mrs Black is Maggie around?"Mrs Black was clearing up the tables."Maggie told me to tell you that she will be at the Night Owl, so you can find her there." I thought to myself,"Is Maggie crazy? She saw what happened to me the last time I went there.I would rather visit Sandy." I went up, took a shower,got dressed, took my camera and left. Mr Black was sitting on the porch peeling peaches with his wife.They looked so happy.I took out my camera and shot them a picture.Time I started creating memories of my own.

Sandy was sitting outside taking a smoke break when I got to Cuppa Jack."Hey you, back for more drinks with uncle Stephan?" I just laughed.

"Can I smoke too?" Sandy took out a smoke for me."Just kidding Sandy, I don't smoke."

"Funny hey Brooks, well how was your jogging with my dad?" I looked across the street and saw my uncle Stephen coming towards us."I enjoyed it so much.I even saw the wine factory.This place is awesome."Sandy showed my eyes in great uncle Stephen's direction."Here comes another drinking time Brooks." I shook my head and said"Not today Sandy." Then I asked"Hey Sandy, who owns the winery?" She smiled and said,"The Blacks."Then she got up and went inside Cuppa Jack.

That wasn't the answer I needed.It's gonna lead me to more questions.My great uncle Stephen was in front of me and greeted me with a warm hug."Bucket I am just here to collect your great aunt Tammy's order.Follow me back to my house when I come out."

I sat outside and waited for him.My phone rang and it was Jones on the line."Hi Brooks my man.I didn't get your report yet as promised?"Chucks I have been so busy I forgot."Hey man, I will send it today."

I am so busy here I need to find a way or someone that can help me do the reports daily.Who can I get.What I need to do is just create a generic template,like a form with all the necessary questions and get the person to ask these questions to clients or individuals or I can even pass them out or ask Sandy to help me and Bridget.Yes problem solved.? Sandy can just put them in her shop and Bridget in the library.I will collect them daily and type them on my computer and send them to Jones.Now that, that's sorted I can go digging.My great uncle Stephen came out with a paper bag full of food and said.``I got you some,my boy.Leave your car here, we will take mine.

Sandy will keep an eye on it my son, your uncle Paul will drop you here if I am not tired." I took the paper bag from him and we walked to the car.It was a very nice SUV with white leather seats and GPS.The inside smelled of cologne and raspberries.We sped of down the direction of The Night Owl.By 200 meters before the Owl we turned right into a road that looked like a farmhouse ahead.Massive place indeed.Stephen pressed a remote control and the gates swung open.This place had swimming pools.I mean 3 of them,a tennis court and basketball court.Areas to relax and have a cookout next to the pools and horses. We got welcomed at the door by Stephens wife and she hugged me and said" You look just like your great-grandfather.Come in my boy.`` The house had staircases going up left and right.Stephen had a huge collection of firearms in glass display cabinets and I could see he is a hunter by the awards and stuffed animals on the walls.There was a wall for the Brooks family only and as I looked closer I saw a picture of me as a baby on the wall.I have the exact same picture.I pointed at the picture and Stephens wife said," Your father sent it when you were born"There was my father as a child and adult.My great-grandfather and his wife Katie.My grandfather William and his brothers Stephen and Doug.There were even pictures of my mother and father on their wedding day and another one of me on my first school day.Amazing.Great uncle Stephen came back with a bottle of whiskey and said" It's your first time in your family home so you are not gonna say no to a welcoming drink.This is where the Brooks legacy began in this same house.This house belonged to my father, your great-grandfather Mr Bucket Brooks and raised us all.I stayed behind with parents in this house because Doug and William got married young and moved out and I felt that someone should stay with the old people. I also moved out later when your father was older and could assist his grandparents.But Preston also moved to the city when he finished school.That broke my parents hearts because they raised him from the first day he was born.So I came back with my wife and our son Paul and after my parents passed on I renovated the whole place and here we are now.I last saw your father when he came here for his grandparents funerals and that was the last time I ever saw him.I saw on the TV News when he was shot and killed.I got sick and slept in hospital for a month.The doctors said I had a minor heart attack.It was Preston's death.I raised that boy when your grandfather William went away with his bride who was not Preston's mother.She only loved her son Isaac the one she had with William. Isaac is the owner of The Night Owl.``I lifted up my hand and stopped uncle Stephen." Please tell me that I am not related to Edmond Yeast?"Stephen laughed and said,"Edmond Yeast is the son of your uncle Isaac's sister in-law,Jane and Edmond and his father doesn't want part of the fued.So don't worry Edmond is a good boy he visits me when he's off from work together with his father Edgar Marx.Edgar was never married to Jane that's why the kids still use Yeast as surname.Isaac is business partners with Thandai's Rockshers sister Yanda.They own the Owl and other businesses together.The Rockshers and Brooks developed some bad blood in the past.And the Yeast family have always been friends with the Rocksher family. More like their slaves.Your grandfather got married to a Yeast knowing our past.William was a very good hearted man.But I think many of his decisions were clouded but his soft heart.William was involved on both sides of the wall.He dated a Rocksher girl and then went to and married a Yeast girl.Yes Willy was something else."

"Uncle Stephen, tell me, do you know where the Rockshers are now?" Uncle Stephen shook his head and said,"My boy we all last saw them when they went to the city and that's that.They never came back here again.Yanda is the only Rocksher here in town left.But she is a very good person.I don't know how she became business partners with your mean uncle Isaac.And Isaac is fighting against the Brooks family, being a Brooks at that time.He is a fool,he stands on his mother's side and fight against his own blood from his father's side.We don't talk or ever greet each other."

The stories in this town are from a Telenovela."Uncle Stephen.When I arrived at the Owl on Sunday Yanda chased me away for showing her my wife Karen's picture who looks just like her.I took out the picture and showed him.

"They do look the same as my boy . What's her name again?" I put the picture back in my wallet and said,"Her name is Karen Grover." Uncle Stephen shook his head and said,"Nope,no Grovers here.But the strange thing is why was Yanda acting so strange towards you my boy?" That was strange to me too.

The whiskey was of top quality and aunt Tammy brought us the food from Cuppa Jack.The people in this place keep feeding me.I am gonna become fat in no time.

"Just one question,Uncle Stephen.Who is my grandmother?"

"Your grandmother, my boy.I don't think we can talk about that now.Its a topic that doesn't sit well with me.Can we discuss that at another time.Come let me show you my horses.?"

I need to find out who my grandmother is and I need someone that can help me find the Rockshers.

We stood watching the horses when Uncle Stephen said,"Did Black tell you he was your father's best friend?"

I just nodded a yes.My mind was racing.I think I should ask Mr Black.

I told my uncle that I had a great time and I needed to get to the Library before they closed.His son was not back yet so he agreed to drop me at Cuppa Jack.Sandy was serving coffee to a man that gave me a stare that's not very welcoming.Maggie was there her car was parked outside but I didn't see her in the shop."Sandy, where is Maggie.I see her car but not her?"The stranger was still staring at me and making me feel very uncomfortable.He was well dressed with an expensive watch and I guessed the expensive sports car outside belonged to him."Maggie is in the bathroom.I looked at the strangers table and saw 2 cups meaning he had company.One of the elderly couples that were there yesterday called me to their table and asked me to sit with them for a few minutes.They introduced themselves as the Shrouder family and Mr Shrouder was the town pastor and Mayor.They spoke about church and marriage and asked about my wife and spoke about how naughty my father and there son Craig and Jack was.I was not interested I hardly listened to a word they said.I was more interested in this stranger and who is joining him at his table.And there she was Maggie.She went straight to the table and sat down besides the stranger.I didn't move and just sat there with the pastor and his wife.Maggie turned around and saw me.She came over and said," I came looking for you and ran into this friend of mine he was just passing through and strangely he met me here.Small world hey?" I just looked at her with my fake smile and said,"Small indeed." I said my goodbyes to the Pastor and his wife and left without saying a word.I need to pass by the Library and see Mr Black again. I got to the Library in time and told Bridget my plans for the daily report at work and she agreed to help me and told me she would type and send them for me too.The library is only busy after school.During the day she does nothing.Bridget my champ.Bridget told me that Edmond send his regards and said he will be here weekend to teach me to ride horses.I drove past the church on the outside route this time and it looked amazing.

Chapter 8
Grandma

I found the Blacks baking in the kitchen and flour and sugar were all over.Mr Black was wearing an apron and dancing all over the kitchen while helping his wife. Mrs Black called me to one side and told Mr Black to check the oven because she wanted to speak to me.

"Brooks my boy.Sit down here." Pointing at a kitchen stool.And handing me a cookie."Brooks you know since you came here Mr Black has been jovial and he enjoys life a little bit more.But I am scared that when you leave he might go into depression like he did when your father died.Mr Black and your father were best friends growing up and they had a big fallout and never spoke again. Preston died and they never made peace.That broke him.I think he is trying to replace Preston with you.I am not saying it's true.But I need you to speak to him,do it very subtly. Please.?" Mr Black came over and asked,"What are you too gossiping about"?.

Mrs Black took a cookie and stuffed it in his mouth and said we are talking about the Gold Annual Dance next week." Mr Black got even more excited."Yes Brooks you can take Sandy to the dance.She hasn't been there for the past 5 years since she broke up with David Kentro.So you can take her Brooks."

Knowing the Blacks I don't think I will have a chance to say no.I agreed and they both smiled from ear to ear.

Sandy was home earlier today and I asked her the same favor I asked Bridget to help with my work report.She agreed to place forms in the shop and get clients to fill them and sign.Sandy told us that she wanted to take a shower before dinner and I helped Mrs Black set up the tables.She kept looking at me and smiled with everything I did I didn't bother to ask Sandy was down and her mother asked her to bring the salads to the table.Maggie was still not home.

After dinner Sandy asked me to join her on the porch and she brought a six pack of beer with her.The moon was high and the sounds of dogs in the distance and barking and crickets sounded like a symphony from nature.Sandy sat beside me and passed me a beer.Mr and Mrs Black were singing their lungs out today inside the house.Sandy told me they would do it once or twice a week.She was used to it.Sandy looked at me and giggled.

"What's wrong with you Sandy?" She giggled again and said."Damn Brooks you don't take your alcohol well hey?" I told her that I haven't heard that before.She almost choked on her beer.

"Brooks, did you see the guy in the shop with Maggie today? That guy told me that he knows you and he was surprised that you don't know him.Maggie told me that they went to school together with your wife."

This was funny because he never came up to me to introduce himself and Maggie never bothered to introduce him too.

"Apparently Maggie and this guy dated for a short period but now they're only friends.They both gave me this strange look when I asked how he knew she was here in the Parish out of all the places in the world.He didn't come here to see anyone for business or a visit and they both left together to see Yanda at the Owl.I think you should keep your mouth shut around Maggie and don't involve her in your plans anymore.At Least give her enough to retain the trust but don't share anymore secrets with her.I think she works for the Rocksher family as a double agent.They are planning something. Maggie wants to use you as the secret weapon because you are so gullible my city friend. Don't worry Brooks, I will keep an eye on her and her new friend." I thanked Sandy for looking out for me.

"Sandy, tell me what you know about my Grandmother?" Sandy almost choked again on her beer.

"Brooks in this town it's not a very good idea to speak about your grandmother.It stirs up bad feelings and it's better left to rest." Why is my grandmother such a big secret.Even Stephen avoided the topic.

"Now just one thing Sandy, is my grandmother still alive?" She took a sip from her beer and said,"The time she left this town she was very much alive." This means I can still find my grandmother. The night was so very relaxed and peaceful. "Another thing Sandy, what was my grandmother's name?" Sandy got irritated with me.

"Brooks, stop this issue please?"

As we sat there Maggie came in through the gate but she was alone.She greeted us and we greeted her back.She went in and never came back.Strangely enough, Maggie wanted me to meet her at the Owl today but she still couldn't tell me why.Now and earlier.She didn't even ask why I never came.Sandy might be on to something regarding her.

"Brooks, you wanted to know about the Rocksher family.And yes my father tells me everything you guys say and do.Let me tell you what I know about them.The Rocksher had 4 generations of family living on that farm and the last was a mixed blood native Kundu .Everyone in this town knew that they were never people to mess around with because the grandfather Tomoko who was some type of spirit man from Africa and he had no friends at all.His family and kids were his friends.The old spirit man was a horse breeder and brilliant at it too. Rocksher and his father and grandfather were all black farmers and his mother white.Makuba married a white woman Miss Naomi Scott who became Rocksher and mother to Kundu.Makuba was brought here with by his father Tomoko at a young age of 4 and he never attended school.He was a hard man.And loved horses.Now Kundu's father Makuba was also a hard man and forced his son to work the land from a young age.Kundu's grandfather Tomoko was a dangerous spirit man and thought his grandson the trade of using dark magic the same as he did with his son Makuba.Kundu's grandmother was killed in

Africa when she was called a witch and burned at the stake.Tomoko got help from some of his white farmer friends,sold his land.He took all the money he had took his young son and moved to the Parish.He bought a piece of land and started breeding horses and planted peaches.He was the first person to plant peaches that you see all over the Parish.Now the Rockshers were not Rocksher before.The Parish community struggled to pronounce their surname Rokosumbakataka and they changed it to Rocksher.The towns people spoke of big snakes spotted on the Rocksher farm ritualistic murders and sightings of witchcraft and black magic,but everyone was afraid to speak up against them."

"Makuba's wife Naomi was believed to have voodoo dolls.She came from a family of white farmers.Her father bought horses from Tomoko and the two kids fell secretly in love and before they knew it Naomi was pregnant and forced to marry Makuba,Tomoko passed away before Kundu was born.Just a month before time.Makuba took over the farm and reign to the wickedness that he and his father practiced and taught it to his wife who became and expert in her own right.Kundu was taught the trade himself.And never allowed to go to school.Kundu married a white woman too like his father her name was Florence Palmer and she was the mother of Thandai and Yanda.Florence went against the will of her father and mother in law and send her kids to school.Which in return benefited this town.Just imagine if Thandai' was a sorcerer like the generations before him he would have never found the gold. But legend has it that Clare who is Thandai's daughter took over the trade of sorcery and was very good at it.In this town people are even afraid to say bad things about the Rockshers.They have told of stories were the spirit of Tomoko strangled people to death and people even caught fire when mentioning their names.Some say that they see Naomi sitting at the farm gate at night next to a fire.Nobody goes to the old farm across the lake that belongs to them.Thandai also married to a white woman it's like they wanted to get all the black out of the family.But the blood still runs in the veins and the evil they posses can still be felt in the atmosphere.Let's go in Brooks it's getting colder now?"

"Sandy, how do you know all these stories?"

"Brooks my friend, some of the things happened before my time and others during my time and everyone in the town knows the history, it's passed on from generation to generation.I am gonna tell you a little secret.The Sunday you came here.Maggie screamed and my father said it was just the trees.I don't think so.I have seen Naomi and Tomoko myself and my father keeps saying it's my imagination.The room Maggie has used to be mine.I even sleep with a Bible and holy water next to my bed.Why do you think I wear so many crosses on my necklace it's not as a fashion statement.This place is dangerous Brooks.Wait and see my friend."

Sandy spoiled my whole mood.Just when I thought Firthlink was bad.I came right into the Dragon's mouth.

But now that I am here I think destiny has a plan for me.I need to get to the old Rocksher farm.Maybe I can find something.But who will be brave enough to go with me.I think I will have to contact the Blue Boys.They always loved an adventure, but if Fred spoke to them regarding my current situation they might not agree.Maybe the twins will.They were always brave.Sandy grabbed me by the hand and said,"Seriously let's

go to bed?"

Who are you grandmother.Why don't people wanna speak about you.I need to see uncle Stephen again and force the truth out of him.He needs to tell me atleast her name.I need to get something.Now it's becoming clear that the spirit in my house in Firthlink has something to do with the Rockshers.But why me and what did I do that it's after me.Or is it something to do with the history of this town and the bad blood between the families.I am gonna find out what these people are hiding from me and why this spirit is after me.Why can't this spirit attack any of the Brooks family.Why me? Why? I was so happy for these past 3 days but now I am back to square one.Let me rather sleep.Grandmother please come back to me if you are still alive.I need to find out who I am? Finding my grandmother, means finding the link to my past.

Chapter 9
Preston Brooks

The following morning I woke Mr Black up myself for our morning jog.

"Brooks, it's too early to go back to bed."I kept knocking on his door and I wasn't going away.

"Ok,ok,I am coming Brooksie." I could hear Mrs Black chuckling from the bedroom."Come on Mr Black, this is the best time to hit the road in the morning." Mr Black came out and punched me on the arm and said,"Irritating just like your father, let's go?" I smiled from behind him.We took our same route and the atmosphere showed that winter was coming to an end. It wasn't as cold anymore.Maybe a few days are left of winter.But honestly speaking our winters are not as cold as other places.Mr Black looked tired today."Brooks, Brooks.We are not taking 2 laps today, one is enough.We took our lap and sat on our log same as yesterday."Mr Black , is there anyone living there?"Pointing at the Rocksher farm. He gave me a wide eyed look and said."Boy don't test me.Don't you dare try to go there.I will be very angry with you and I don't want to lose you too like I lost your father." Mr Black had a very serious look in his eyes.A mixture of scared and angry."I mean it Brooks."

I agreed with my mouth, but I knew in my heart I was going there.I just have to keep it a secret from him.

"By the way Mr Black.I need to know about you and my father and what led to your fight?"Mr Black got up from the log and walked away from me."Sorry Mr Black.I didn't mean to make you upset."He turned back and said,"It's not your fault.And you deserve the truth." He came back and sat next to me."Well where do I begin my boy.Preston and I go back from first grade and Sunday School.We did everything together and went everywhere as a pair.We could share everything and confided in each other about everything.They called us brothers.We even dressed the same."

This made me think about Fred.I miss him.

"Well it all started with a certain girl here in town.We both liked that girl.But the girl liked Preston even more.I tried everything to get the girl but it didn't work.At that time Preston was in a relationship with another girl named Freda Bloom.The one that owns Bloom Grocery Store.Well Freda was a bit of a cheater and Preston liked her but he also had his eye on the other girl we both fancied.I felt your was standing in my way to be with this girl while he had Freda.I became jealous because he has 2 and I had none.Freda was playing around and Preston was standing in my way and I had to do something.My father owned a old Valiant with white wall tires and it was the envy of many.My father never wanted to sell that car even after many offers and called her Brown Sugar.Maybe because of her brown color.The school dance was coming up and I didn't have a date.

Preston broke up with Freda and asked this girl to the dance.The girl agreed and I was out of a chance to get the girl of my dreams again.I needed to come up with a plan and I had the perfect one.I told Preston that since I had no partner for the dance I would borrow him Brown Sugar.I told him that my father agreed to me using the car and gave Preston the keys.Since my parents were out of town Preston couldn't ask them if it was true or not.I turned and called the police and told them my father's car was stolen.They found Preston driving the car and I denied giving him the car.I got to comfort the girl while Preston spend the night in prison.I told the police and the girl that he is my friend and had freedom to my house.So he came in a took the keys and drove off with the car."

I looked at the old man next to me and almost punched him.Ler me continue listening."Well my father came back yesterday and dropped the charges because he knew Preston and he was very angry at me for what I did and when he found out I did all this for a girl he got more angry and said he hopes this girl is worth destroying my friendship.Now this girl found out what I had done and was angry at me too.Preston was no longer interested in this girl or me and he was just angry at the world.I was the cause of it all.The girl forgave me and we started seeing each other.

But Preston refused.He became friends with Craig Shrouder.He is the son of the Pastor.They became close friends and I felt left out.I missed Preston but he looked at me like a bug needed to be squashed. I had my girl but lost my brother.On a faithful Christmas about a year after my fall out with your father we walked into each other at the Church and the seats left were next to each other.The Sunday school kids had their own play on stage about Christmas and kept forgetting their lines.It was hilarious and we got to talking about our first play.We laughed and chatted.Maybe it was the Church atmosphere or something.But we went home being friends again,just like that your father forgave me.He took a year to forgive me after many attempts and in just a few minutes in church he did.We became a trio with Craig and boy did we get up to mischief.The following year went to University because that's a must in this town.Since from the time of the mining trio."

"We all enrolled at the same University and did almost the same courses just to be together all the time.I still dated the girl and our relationship was no longer an issue to anyone.Even your father.Our friendship got stronger and after University started our own company together.We assisted the mine with safety,security and healthy matters on a consultancy basis.We did very well as a firm.We wanted to become business magnets just like our fathers.One day we sat just like you and me on this same spot.And your father said "Jackson, what do you see on that farm?"

"Yes my full name is Jackson."I just smiled at Mr Black..

"I said there is nothing I see.And he said look closely.I told him peaches a lot of them.Preston said yes Black we can turn it into a business.Your father wanted us to get a place and start manufacturing food products that uses peaches.That was a good idea because the peaches were everywhere.But we needed a premises to start and we didn't have one.I spoke to my father and he agreed to assist us.Well your grandfather William and my father had land that they bought a long time ago and planned to build a hotel and Truck stop there.Your grandfather was not interested in a Truck Stop anymore and when my father presented a new business plan he jumped on the wagon.My father convinced me and talked me into becoming a partner in his scheme.Only they didn't want me to tell Preston because they knew he wouldn't approve.Me, William and my father started the winery and Preston was left outside again.The winery made more money than what the food products would have.

William knew that Preston hated alcohol and would never agree to a winery so that was the reason to cut him out of the deal. The winery turned the town's people into angry drunks and a lot of things started going wrong because people had a lot of money coming from the mine and time on their hands so they drank and drank. Preston hated me all over again and this time he didn't want to fix things between us.William tried speaking to his son.Preston forgave his father and my father.But hated me for not having the guts to be honest about the winery.Your father decided to leave this town and never come back again.The winery makes a lot of profits even now and your father sold his shares to Yanda Rocksher."

"So Mr Black what happened to the girl you and my father fought over."

Mr Black gave me a small giggle and said,"She became Sandy's mother.And she has been my first and only love until now.Mrs Pearl Black is that girl my boy."

True love I guess?

Mr Black got up and said," Lets go slugger?" We jogged slowly back to the B&B and found Mrs Black at the gate going out."Boys make yourself something to eat I am going out to the beauty salon for my hair and nails.Want to prepare for the dance this Saturday.You boys be good now.And Jack, take Brooks out for some shopping he needs to look good for the dance.I already told Sandy and she agreed to go with Brooks to the dance?"

We went in and I told Mr Black that I needed to take a shower and he told me that he needed one too.After my shower I got into my room and found 25 missed calls on my phone and it's all from Fred.Since I have been here Karen hasn't returned my calls or replied to any of my messages and I think I should give her some space. I will call Fred after breakfast.I don't want to hear anything that would spoil my appetite now.I went downstairs and found that Mr Black had already made some eggs and toast for us.I sat down and he put some sauces on the table too.

"Bucket, I loved your father as my own blood and I wish I could undo the wrongs of the past.I live with the pain all my life and it's too late now to ask for his forgiveness.I wish you can find it in your heart to forgive an old fool for the sins of the past.When I saw you I knew that this was my chance at redemption.An opportunity to fix what I broke and heal in the same process.I live with an emptiness that only forgiveness can heal.So please forgive me?"

I got up and gave him a hug with tears flowing down his eyes.I felt so sorry for Mr Black."Mr Black we are not perfect there are people that have done far worse.We will get past this."

Chapter 10
Glen and Bruno

I thanked Mr Black for breakfast and told him that I am just going out to the porch to make a phone call to a friend at home."Hello,hello."Fred took his own time to answer.And when he did,it sounded like,"Oh,oh man Pete oh my word.Man it's bad.Its real bad.The guys, Pete the guys,oh man." I told Fred to calm down and start explaining everything slower.

He was stuttering immensely and I could hear the sound of his teeth clattering together.Fred was really shaken up."Pete, they are all dead.Dead Pete."

"Who is dead Fred?" Fred started crying and I begged him to stop.He started speaking again.

"Pete,Bruno and Glen are dead. The neighbors heard a lot of noise coming from your house last night.Screaming and groaning sounds coming from.The neighbors said it sounded like a beast attacking them and they called the police.The police got to the house but they couldn't get in.The screaming continued for the whole night.It seems that something was locking the doors and entrances from the inside.When they eventually managed to get in.They were met with horrifying scenes.Blood, bones, hair and flesh all over the house.The worst part that the eyes and internal organs are all gone.Karen is the one that called me.Apparently she told me that she didn't get hold of you and asked me to pass the message.The neighbors gave the police her contact numbers."

Is it strange that I send Karen messages and calls all the time and she doesn't say anything?And then she sends Fred as my messanger.I don't even wanna know how I am gonna explain this one.This spirit is really angry and getting out of control.

"Pete your house is a crime scene.The police want a statement from me and you.Karen and I told them you went away with work but they still need to speak to you so expect a call from them.The police report states, there was no sign of forced entrance but they need to know from us what those 2 men were doing in your house and the pest control guy doesn't want anything to do with this matter he told the police that we hired them for pest control and they know nothing about Bruno or Glen."

How am I gonna get myself out of this one.Fred and I are not guilty.The pop police will prove that but Karen is aware of what's happening now or at least she will find out.

"Pete the scene was horrific.Splatters of blood painted the ceilings and walls.Gaping holes are distributed all over the walls and floors.The holes appear to be created by some type of construction machine, digging deep into the canvas.Broken furniture and blood baths decorate the floors. The carcasses of the two men have no bone in them left intact.They are dried out from all body fluids and they looked like they got sucked by some pressure compressor machine.

It appears that they got dragged from room to room and beaten against the canvases, indicating where the gaping holes originate from.Their demise was most unpleasant.I don't wish that on my worst enemy and it pains me Pete to know we put them in that situation and it's only getting started.The police recovered video tapes and sound recordings on the scene.It's been kept as evidence and I have a connection in the force that promised to get me copies.We need to find out what Glen and Bruno discovered before they were so brutalized."

"The neighbors are traumatized and moved away today until the police get to the bottom of this crazy unnatural occurrence at your house.I feel the need to do the same Pete.I don't want to find or place my family in the crossfire of some supernatural war with an unknown entity that may consume our souls and use our bodies as a decorations for it's evil gratification or satisfaction.I fear Pete that this spirit will start attacking from outside the boundaries of your house and start searching amongst inhabitants of Firthlink that has a connection to you and venture on a hunting spree elementing any individual on it's path. Any one that reeks of Pete can be a target,so I prefer to open up as much distance between me and it Pete."

Fred has a great point.This entity will start searching from outside the premises of my home and find victims that can assist it to search out its prime target.Me.The issue concerning Karen is what grips my mind in a lock and I am dumb found on how to address this issue with her.What if I tell Karen everything and she leads this entity to me and what if I decide to do the opposite and Karen gets devoured.I need to find a way of testing my theory but what?

"Pete, how are you getting along with your investigations?"

I told Fred everything that I have discovered so far in Levensdown.He was shocked to find out that my ancestors are from the same place with the Rocksher family and all my heritage lies here. Fred's blood pressure rose even higher when I told him about the Rocksher history with sorcery and dark spirits.

"Fred, I think you can come here with your family or go to Franklin or one of the Blue Boys.And here you may be able to assist me with my investigations and we can perhaps find a way to beat this spirit.?"

Fred kept quiet for a second and said,"Pete I think I would rather go somewhere else where we don't know a soul. I don't want to put more people I know and love in more danger.I will make sure as soon as I get everything over and done with the police,I run Pete.I will make sure that my contact in the police provide me with copies of all sound recordings and videos, Bruno and Glen managed to obtain.Your neighbors told the police that the voices that came from your house sounded very terrifying.They said it sounded like demonic beasts tearing the men apart.Nothing like this could be human at all.I won't be able to sleep for day's Pete, graphical images are engraved in my memory and will remain there for as long as you my existence remain on this earth."

Fred is going through all this suffering because of me.How can I ever be able to make up for all his agony.My personal problems or perhaps bad life and choices or the bad history of my ancestors and their past sins has returned in the form of a demonic killing machine and the innocent like Fred is caught in this crossfire of death and pure evil,and all you can do if you don't have a solution is run.Run but, to where and for how long?I need to risk everything now to find out how to deal with this entity before more innocent people die.Levensdown must have something or someone that can assist me.Someone needs to know how to fight this thing and I feel that my grandmother can be a link to this issue.Why is she such a big secret in this town.I need to find her before the voices find me.

"Fred, I will wait for the police to call me today and I will tell them the truth about everything that happens in that house.I don't think we have any openings anymore Fred. I believe that if the police present this to Karen she might be more understanding and lenient towards me.I think that she rather look at me as coward that ran away from this problem.This way I will be able to see where the Karen stand in this matter.If she works with this thing or of this thing controls her I will be able to see everything now that she knows I know about this thing.If Karen is involved Fred, she and this thing will come after me.I need to prepare Fred because war is coming my way.I will need everything I can and find out everything about what I am dealing with in order to survive.Please take care of your family Fred and be safe my brother."

Fred said his goodbyes and dropped the call.

I went back into the house and found Mr Black having another cup of coffee."Want one Brooks?" Pointing at the kettle."Sure Mr Black I would love it, thank you."I need this old man to open up to me and tell me the truth about my grandmother. I believe she is the missing link or atleast lead me in the correct direction.I need to tell Mr Black everything and if he realizes that my life is in danger he will assist me.I need to play on his feelings.He doesn't want to lose my father again.And by losing me he will lose him again.Send him on a guilt trip.

My phone rang again while me and Mr Black sat at the table."Busy man today Brooks?"I took a sip from my coffee and said,"It's Sandy." Mr Black smiled a slick one for that matter."Hey Sandy, what's cooking?"

"Brooks, you remember the guy that had coffee with Maggie the last time?"I said yes.

"Well that guy was here just now and he was looking for you.I refused to give him your numbers and I told him I will speak to you and convey the message.He left his number and asked that you call him.He said it's urgent and a matter of life and death." Who is this man and what does he want from me?I will have to find out but I need someone to accompany me.And we need to meet in a public place where he won't try something funny."Ok Sandy please forward me his numbers I will contact him?"

I could hear in the sound of Sandy's voice that she was not very sure I should call this guy.``Brooks if you decide to meet this guy anywhere,I am going with you, ok?" The manner in which she said ok, meant she already made a decision for me and I had no way out but to agree.As a matter of fact she just made things easy for me because I was thinking about who to ask to accompany me if I needed to see this guy and here comes the psychic Sandy and reads my mind.I agreed instantly. Mr Black was looking at me with widened eyes and baited breath.``What did Sandy say?" I just smiled at this nosey old man.``She told me someone from the city came looking for me at Cuppa Jack.She sent me the person's contact numbers." Mr Black just nodded with a disappointing look on his face.Was this old man expecting something else.Why do I get a feeling that Jackson Black and Pearl Black are trying to play matchmaker here.Did they forget that I am a married man and my wife might be in danger somewhere.? Mr Black got up said,"Call that person before you go mad.And don't forget we are going shopping later, you and I." Mr Black won't let me escape the dance on Saturday.No matter what and I don't want to disappoint Sandy too.And the dance might provide me with an unlocked opportunity to meet many of the town people and get answers to s few of questions and Edmond will be here.I believe he can be of great assistance.I went out again to call the number Sandy had given me and dialed the number.The phone just rang.I called again and same.Just when I wanted to call again,my phone rang.It was him."Hello, saw two of your missed calls on my phone and I called back.Who am I speaking to?"I sat down on the bench in front of me on the porch because I didn't know how long this call might take.``I am the person you came looking for at Cuppa Jack today."He kept quiet for a second and said,"Okay Mr Brooks."I said yes and asked what he wanted. "Mr Brooks there's some things that I need to discuss with you and I am afraid to speak over the phone.Someone might be listed in our conversations.I there a place we can meet Mr Brooks, apart from Cuppa Jack I think people are watching me there." I thought about somewhere and then I remembered the library is empty this time of the day and Bridget can be trusted."Before I agree to meet you.How do I know that I can trust you.I know nothing about you Mr.And the last time I saw you, you didn't greet me or even speak to me.So how do you think I should trust you?"He paused and said my name is Gold. Zane Gold." Damn this is the name that appeared on the paperwork Karen always brought to me to sign when we bought our house.So just like Sandy told me ,according to Maggie these guys all go back to school years with Karen.But why does he want to meet in private and why is he so scared to be seen with me? Either way I need to hear what he has to say.I told Zane to meet me at the library in an hour and I called Sandy to meet me there.Sandy agreed to close the shop and meet me at least 20 minutes before Zane arrives so we can scout the area for any surprises from him.

I told Mr Black that I am going out to see Sandy and I will be back for our shopping trip.

Sandy and I got there and asked Bridget to lend us one of the offices for our meeting,and to check for Zane when he comes through and direct him to where we're waiting.

Exactly 13h00 he came through.I tried to remember if I have seen this guy anywhere before apart from Cuppa Jack but the answer was,no I have never seen him.He dressed very well and had a serious look on his face like a army drill soldier.You could see that this type of guy hardly ever smiled.He was all business.But what does Mr Serious want from me.?He greeted us and sat down. I was honest with him and told him that I called Sandy to the meeting because I don't trust him and I still don't.He assured me that he was not my enemy, in fact he told me that he was here to help me instead.

"Mr Brooks you don't know me but I know you. Karen, Maggie and I go back years and attended the same University.I am also related to Jimmy Colby. Our mothers are sisters.Story short,I went to Firthlink looking for you and Jimmy pointed me to Fred who told me where to find you."Sandy turned to me with skeptical eyes but she kept quiet.

"So Mr Brooks, I came here looking for you.Strangely I found Maggie here and I couldn't say anything to you because I don't trust her and neither should you Mr Brooks." I agreed.I couldn't think what he was about to tell me would shake my world.``Mr Brooks I am sure when you and Karen bought your house, you always saw my name on the paperwork.I am sure you trusted your wife enough and never bothered to ask about me. Well Mr Brooks.I am a lawyer but I also have a Real Estate company and Karen approached me because she knew she could trust me.She told me that you guys got married and you were looking for property to buy.I showed her many different properties ,but she wasn't interested.Mr Brook, Karen always told me you were busy when I asked about you and I never really got bothered by the idea, because in the end she was your wife and I believed you trusted her completely.The strange thing is that I took Karen to different properties,much cheaper and bigger and closer to many commodities but she wasn't interested.There were many other offers for the Rocksher mansion by other individuals and Karen made sure her price was higher everytime.Karen was only interested in the Rocksher house from day one and nothing else.I questioned this when I was alone but let it slide.Being a businessman and receiving a big commission was all I could see.But there was one thing that really got me thinking and scared is when we had to sign the transfer paperwork from the previous owners, Karen told me that she will get that sorted out and I shouldn't worry because she knows the owners and will get them to sign.Strangely enough Mr Brooks.Nobody knows where the Rocksher family is.How would she be able to get them to sign?"

This Zane Gold has just refreshed my memory. I just remembered seeing the name Emily Rocksher under owner on the paperwork.All these things happened in front of my eyes,her real name and what Maggie's doing here.I need to track her movement.?

"Mr Brooks, they didn't mention any names it's like they spoke in code.I could gather onething Mr Brooks and that is Karen was very wealthy and I believed that she was using an alias and Karen wasn't her real name.I also heard Maggie ask about you and Karen said she will deal with you when the time is right.I am happy that I found you Mr Brooks and I am here to help you get to the bottom of everything.But we need to pretend that we don't know each other and keep everything on the hush I don't want them to know that I know their wicked plan.I want to stay close to Karen and get as much info and you stick to Maggie.We need to find the Rockshers and we will get to the bottom of this." Sandy saw my eyes fill up with tears and put her hand around me and held me tight.I couldn't help and I let go.Tears just started flowing from the sockets of my eyes.I cried for not knowing who I really was,I cried for suffering for the sins of the past and I cried for loving Karen so much.I was in love with a stranger that's planning bad things for me and my life is just crumbling in front of my eyes and I can't do anything.I just Zane just sat there speechless and I could see him feeling bad for the matter in which I cried and I could see he felt responsible for this.He kept apologizing and I kept breaking down.My tears got interrupted by my phone ringing.It was Karen.I showed Sandy and Zane and they told me to answer and put it on speaker.I cleared my voice and answered.

"Hi honey, how are you?" Karen sounded like someone driving."Babe,I am ok and where are you,I miss you and I plan to come to you.I put in some leave days?" Zane looked at me and shook his head."Honey I don't stay in one place I travel daily so it won't be a good idea for us to be together now.You enjoy sleeping late when you're home and in hotel rooms that won't work." I could hear her sigh."Ok Pete see you when you get back." Things are getting out of control.

"Zane I am sure Maggie gave Karen the details of where I am at and I am sure she is coming here.We need to come up with a plan?" Zane agreed.

"You know guys Maggie pretended so much about being a good person and trying to help me,all along knowing who I was an pretending to be my friend.She wanted to invite me to the Night Owl and never told me why and she knew I had a bad first experience there.Why did she want to lure me out?" Sandy looked very scared I could see it in her eyes.She started speaking and I could hear the fear in her voice."Brooks I think Zane should leave the town because they could put one and one together.And Zane you should go and find out about the Rocksher family's whereabouts.Make up a story that would scare Karen just to get information.You are a lawyer think of something.And Brooks you stay here,if Karen comes here we will get the proof needed that she has been behind everything from the start. I have some ideas of my own.Make sure you hide for a day or two Brooks so I can find out what Karen and Maggie is planning.Go to your great uncle Stephen and tell him the truth I am sure he can come up with a plan.Hide your car and everything and I will clear your room at the B&B to derail them into believing you left town.And don't use your numbers get another sim card and don't send emails or anything from your computer.I will contact your office myself and tell Jones the problem.I will make sure I get him to keep everything under wraps.Nobody even at your office has to communicate anything to Karen until we get to the bottom of everything.And ask Fred to keep quiet to anyone asking about you.And you Mr Gold please don't involve anyone.What you find out reaches Brooks only and nobody else.Dont trust anyone guys.Brooks we need to sit down with my parents and give them the heads up."

Zane and I agreed on everything Sandy spoke about."Sandy, what about the dance on Saturday?" She just gave me a smile and said."Brooks we have a date and you're not gonna stand me up."

Zane made left us at the Library and told me that I should send him the new numbers I will be using.He didn't waste any time and went straight to the Owl were he was booked into and he made sure everyone saw him leave town even Maggie that was having a drink there as strange as always.I went back to the B&B and Sandy went back to Cuppa Jack.Mr Black was busy wiping off his car."I was just about to call you Brooks.Are you ready for our shopping trip?" This old man is always optimistic.``Mr Black before we go I need you to accompany me to my great uncle Stephen first.There is something I need to discuss with both of you?" I just went up, took my bags and laptop and gave the keys to Mr Black."Why are you taking your bags Brooks and why are you handing me the keys to your room?" Mr Black looked worried.``Don't worry Mr Black.We will discuss everything when we reach Stephen's house.I don't want us to talk here.Follow me from behind old man?" He didn't like that.``Who's an old man boy?"

We got to great uncle Stephen and he let us in.I drove right around to the back of the house and he asked me why I am parking the car so far.I asked him and Mr Black to come in with me because I needed to speak to them urgently.My great aunt was busy making food and asked if we will be joining them.Mr Black told her that we still had to be somewhere today so we won't be able to join them.I told my uncle and Mr Black everything and my aunt sat there listening and when I was done she got up and said."Stephen it's time you old man tell the boy the whole truth and nothing but the truth.I believe it's time.Can you guys see that things are getting out of control now?"

The two old men just dropped their heads into their hands and said they can't tell me because it will bring back the past that has been buried so long."Stephen and Jackson, can't you see that the past is back and it's coming for this boy.This boy needs to know the truth now?" What is so big that these old men are hiding from me? I will get the truth like it or not.

Chapter 11
Truth or truth

My great uncle looked at Mr Black and said,"Jackie I don't know how to tell this boy everything.We have had peace in this town for years now and now you come back Bucket and you stir up a demon that was quiet for a long time.Why did you have to come back my boy.Why?" Is this old man even listening to himself speak.Is he drunk or just selfish.And before I could say something his wife jumped in and said,"You are a very selfish old man Stephen.Bucket is your blood and he came here for help because the evil of this town is chasing after him now and you think about yourself.You and the people of this town contributed to this evil and now this boy must suffer on his own.That's wrong." Mr Black agreed with my great aunt.Uncle Stephen got up and poured himself a stiff shot of whiskey,downed it and poured a second and walked back to his seat." Guys anyone that needs one go ahead.Well Bucket my boy I agree with your great aunt.It's time for the truth."He drank his second shot and started speaking."Bucket I wasn't entirely honest with you my boy.It was about the Rocksher family and Tandai's parents and why the Thandai left this town.Thandai's father Kundu and his mother Florence Palmer were very wicked people like the generations before them.Well Florence was the illegitimate child of Farmer Hughes.And Mr Palmer never knew that because Mrs Palmer kept it a secret from her husband but Florence knew as she caught her mother and Farmer Hughes in the act twice and they begged her not to tell Mr Palmer and got her to swear on secrecy.Now Florence also heard them speak about her paternity and she knew Mr Hughes was her father but she never told anyone.Florence worked at the Hughes Heights as a maid and Farmer Hughes and his wife treated her very badly.Mr Hughes knew she was his child but that didn't change his wicked heart.He still regarded Florence as nothing and showed it in his treatment towards her and Florence hated him.Florence hated her mother as much as she hated farmer Hughes and she wanted to find her revenge but she didn't know how.Kundu saw Florence working at the Hughes farm when he went with his father Makuba to check on a horse they sold to the Hughes and he fell in love with her on first sight and made it his mission to marry her and he succeeded.Florence couldn't take the life on Hughes Heights any more and marriage to a black farmer was better than hell on a white farm.Well Florence had her mother in law on the Rocksher farm,Naomi who was deep into the practice of dark sorcery and introduced Florence into this dark world of demonic spirits and spirits.Florence with an already dark heart easily welcomed this new power and felt it was the right tools she needed for her revenge.

Mr Black got up and poured himself a drink too and I asked for one too."Mr Black said."Continue Stevie.It's time we talked." He handed me my drink."Well Bucket my boy, Florence and her mother inlaw became very close in and became very strong and dangerous sorcerers they even had a following and helped many people through darkness.Many of which are still secret followers even now.Thats what I told you that we can't just mention the name Rocksher anywhere in this town.Now the first person that was consulted regarding the plan to purchase the Hughes farm was Mrs Florence Rocksher and her mother in law.I need to be honest you Bucket.When my father,Mr Black and Thandai Rocksher wanted to purchase the farm they spoke to Florence when they needed the money that was short for the sale to go through.Instead of providing them with money, Florence gave them something else.And yes my boy Brooks I lied when I said they sold everything they owned to raise the money that was short.Florence gave them each a potion to rub on and told them to look Mr Hughes straight in the eyes and he will agree on the price.When asked about Mrs Hughes, Florence told her grandson and his friends that Mrs Hughes will agree on anything Mr Hughes say."

This is getting really serious and I got up to pour another drink and the old men asked for more too.

"Brooks my boy," Mr Black said, holding his glass out towards me."We are all victims of some deal our parents made with the devil and now this devil wants more than the agreement price.What Stephen is saying is all true.Florence gave our fathers the potion and yes it worked and they got the farm.But what Florence never told them is by them making contact with Mr Hughes while using the potion will actually put a spell on Mr Hughes that will put him under her and Naomi's control.She used the 3 as couriers and they didn't find out until years later.Florence and Naomi lured the Hughes out to the Rocksher farm together with her own mother Mrs Palmer and used them as sacrificial lambs for a ritualistic offering.The bodies were never discovered and nothing could be proven but our fathers knew and kept everything a secret out of Thandai spoke of his mother and grandmother together with his father and grandfather eating human organs that they stored in jars and in freezers.Thandai wanted to run but he was afraid of their powers.With all the money Thandai made he was still under their control.In this town people started disappearing and people were found with organs missing,but nothing could be pointed at the Rockshers because they had money and sorcery.The town people decided to form an attack on them and people disappeared even more.Some people even mentioned a giant snake on the farm that they prayed to and those people were never to be seen again.Enough was enough and we had to find a way on the farm.But we couldn't risk Thandai's family he just gotten the married and had a young wife and baby on the way and they already suspected especially when he bought a house and moved out.Florence loved her son Thandai and didn't want anyone to hurt her son no matter what.She was prepared to die for him even if he was called a traitor in his family.Florence was the one that encouraged her son move out because she could see the plans to get him killed or placed under a spell to control him was quickly drawing closer.Time went past and Thandai and our fathers became big businessmen and had wives and kids.And people kept disappearing in this town and even speaking about the Rocksher family became a risk.There were dark forces around every corner spying and lurking.People got afraid of walking the streets at night and everyone was afraid to stand up to them."

Uncle Stephen started speaking again.

"We decided that we needed a spy on the inside,but the Rockshers didn't want any employees or friends and our only ally, Thandai was on the blacklist.Even the children living on the farm attended boarding schools and didn't have friends in the town,accept for Thandai,he never wanted to be part of his family's wickedness.We were young boys one-day sitting here on the Brooks property and William came in with a smile on his face.He told me that he just saw an angel and think he is in love. Jackson was not even born at that time.I was about 20 years of age.Jackson here was born in that same year.I think Mr Black was a little slower than Bucket and Thandai."

I could see Mr Black didn't like that remark from my uncle.

"Well I was very interested to know who the girl was and William told me that he doesn't know her name but they would meet again tomorrow at the Library.About a month went by and William kept meeting with his secret girl.Until he came back one-day and was scared out of his wits.He didn't want to talk about it until a week passed and when I gave up on asking he said Stephen do you know that the girl I am in love with is a Rocksher and she is only 13 years of age.She doesn't look 13 and she lied about her age.William was 18 years old at that time and this could spell problems with the law.But the more William opened up a gap between him and this girl.The closer she wanted to be with my brother William.She would come here on weekends and days she was off from boarding school and William gave in on her charms and consistency,and dated her in secret.They dated for a year or two in secret and William and this girl begged me not to tell anyone she was a Rocksher because she didn't want to be treated like an outcast.I could see she and William loved each other and we're happy.But things were about to turn very sour for all of us.The disappearing of people became worse and we had to do something urgently.Mr Shrouder who just became the town pastor came up with a plan.He decided that in order to win over evil we needed to find the good and faithful.He recruited people from different backgrounds.People of the clergy,men and women military and police backgrounds and even people that have practice dark magic before.They called themselves " The Senate".All 21 of them. With all the expertise and armed muscle they had.It was still a difficult mission and more people died.People got found cut up in pieces in the graveyard.Body parts got found drifting on the lake.Law enforcement from different states came and searched the Rocksher farm but nothing was ever found.It was clean.The grounds were dug up for corpses but nothing.Something had to give.Then came the breakthrough.The girl dating William had information on how to break the power of the Rockshers.She found out that her family has an amulet on the farm.Hidden somewhere.That amulet accompanied by a certain spell and ritual can break the power they have.By doing this they can be overpowered.Williams girl loved him so much and wanted a normal life with him and was willing to turn on her family for the sake of love.Now the only way for her to get close to the emulate and understand the spells and rituals.She needed to be part of everything and become a member to this wickedness.It was a risk this girl was prepared to take for love.Months went by and she was busy going through the initiation and passing with flying colors for that matter.Her grandmother was proud of her and promised to protect her all the time."

I could see uncle Stephen sweating now.This story was giving him hot flushes.He paused to wipe his face and then continued again.

"The plan fell into place and the girl managed to get the amulet and the spell.She gave it to the Senate and showed them everything they needed to do.The Senate managed to trap the family on the farm and performed the ritual just as the girl had told them.Now this girl was clever and she knew the days they didn't practice ritualistic activity and she knew the amulet won't be guarded and that's when she took it.The Rockshers were caught off guard and they all got trapped on the farm and dragged of into the woods were they all got burned by the stake.The only ones not burned was Yanda, Thandai and his wife and kids.Months later about 8 months if I am correct the Senate went back to the farm to search around and they found the shedded skin of a giant snake but the snake was never found."I looked at my uncle Stephen and turned to Mr Black and I had to ask,"Now if you say Yanda and Thandai survived with Thandai's kids,Evan, June and Clare and Helga, Thandai's wife,than what about William's girlfriend?" Just as Stephen was about to talk Yanda walked through the door.I almost fell over.What was she doing here at the Brooks home?She greeted everyone and as said,"Stephen we have to cancel the dance this Saturday.Five members of the Senate came to see me today and told me it is happening again.The evil is back and they killed two members in Firthlink at the house of this boy",as she pointed at me.So Yanda knows who I am but why did she she act so weird the first time we met? She started speaking again.``Stephen did you tell this boy everything, I mean everything?"Uncle Stephen shook his head and she said.``Boy let me tell you who and what you are.My younger brother Thandai left this town because of the wickedness of my family.I was lucky by the time everything happened I wasn't even living here.So even when I came back people welcomed me because they knew that Thandai and I were good people.Our parents and grandparents were evil doers and had the blood of generations of evil within them.Thandai and I managed to break the cycle and chose a different path.Now I know you are asking yourself why I acted funny when I met you and why I chased you away.My family the Rockshers had disciples of their own who are still practicing darkness in secret and I wanted to protect you by chasing you away.And I am sure you want to know about Maggie.I found out that Maggie is a disciple and also related to your wife Karen.Now Maggie has been following you all the time from Firthlink and you never noticed.I called her to the Owl because I wanted to scrub her tongue and she trusted me because of my surname thinking I am also a disciple.Now my boy we need to tell you everything and get you to safety because what I heard is that they are after you and I think we need to tell you who you as are before everything gets more messed up."

Just as Yanda was about to speak my phone rang. It was Zane Gold.I sent him my new numbers before we left the B&B."Hey Zane, what's happening?" He sounded excited on the other side of the line."Mr Brooks you won't believe I got a friend of mine in Africa and guess what,he found the previous owners of your house.Mr Thomas Rocksher and his wife and Eldest son and daughter.The youngest daughter is the one that they don't have contact with and said they haven't spoken to her in 7 years and they can't trace her because there's no records of her on the system.They asked for your numbers and promised to call you soon." I thanked Zane and dropped the call.Zane is good he left today and already he got a lead.I went back in and told them what had just come through.Yanda didn't look surprised.``Bucket I knew Thomas and his family is alive in Africa.He went over there to get help on how to destroy this evil for good.He asked me all this time to keep his whereabouts a secret.But he also told me that his youngest daughter Emily came back,but she can't be found on the system because you know why Bucket Brooks? Because she is now called Karen Brooks." I instantly felt weak and my uncle poured me another shot before I fainted." The day you showed me her picture and I chased you away I was hurt and broken all over again to realize that the wickedness of our parents came back to haunt us again.Yes you are married to your own flesh and blood.Your grandfather William had twins with my teenage niece who was 15 years old at that time.The two boys were Thomas and Preston.The Brooks family wanted to take both kids and the Rocksher family wanted to take both.There was a big fight over the kids and the kids were split between the family's.Clare was very young and didn't have any say in the matter.But it broke her and she was dying and becoming bitter inside.Matters got worse when William was forced to marry the Yeast girl who he didn't love just because his parents didn't want to be part of the Rocksher family.So your grandmother is Clare Rocksher and you are sleeping with your own blood which just sickens me to my stomach.I have a feeling that Karen or Emily whichever we want to call her might be a host for a spirit or she might be a new breed of Rocksher evil.I think she changed her name to Karen to make or difficult to trace her.Bucket we are getting a war that's coming this way fast and we gonna need everything we can.``I was feeling very weak and didn't have an answer to this."So where is Clare.Where is my grandmother?" Everyone looked down and Yanda said," Your grandmother went over to Africa with Thomas,his wife Deena and his children Micheal,Lora and Emily,she got deep into voodoo and darkness and soon became very powerful in the community they lived in and people became afraid of her and burned her by the stake too.They said she died screaming Brooks and month later your grandfather William was found strangled to death." The Senate will come and see you today so be prepared for anything."I stopped Yanda before she left and asked "where is uncle Evan and aunt June now?"

She turned around and said," You will see them soon, don't worry."

My perfect life and marriage was all a lie.I am a lie.The thought of me and Karen and everything we had and did just makes me wanna scream.I just wish that Karen or Emily or whatever she calls herself can be a host.Because the thought of he being this evil makes my blood curdle.And know things are worse because I have that same blood in me.i wish I could just cut myself open and drain out that evil in my veins.How am I gonna get through this pain and betrayal and how will this end for everyone?

Chapter 12
Emily

The Senate came to my uncle's house and I refused to go with them.I don't know why but I just did.You won't believe if I told you that the Ricky and Johnny were part of the new recruits for the Senate and they were the ones that send Bruno and Glen to Firthlink after Fred reached out to them.Fred didn't say anything because they asked him not to tell me anything because they feared that they might draw attention to me.Ricky told me that Frankie is ok and is living somewhere in Europe with his family.They told me that they suggested that Fred move there too.It was like a dream to me.These two brothers were my guardian angels growing up and fought all my battles and now they're here again to fight another one for me.Is this their destiny or what do we call it?My great aunt Yanda asked me to make sure I give her a call if I see or make contact with Maggie.I wondered what my uncle Thomas and his family was like and would they accept me in the family.I spoke to my great uncle Stephen when he got a call from Yanda."Brooks ,Emily is in town. I just spoke to her and she was asking about Bucket.Please make sure she doesn't lay an eye on him."Stephen told me what Yanda said and took me to the back of the house where he had a secret room underneath his garage.The Senate was also notified about Emily."A message came through from Fred and it was the recordings and videos from his friends at the police.He told me that he got my new contact from Zane Gold. I opened the videos and what I saw next was truly out of a horror movie.The video showed a dark shadow or shadows grabbing the Bruno and Glen from side to side.Bashing them against the walls and floors and then ripping them open and pulling out their internal organs.The entity then started sucking them dry like a person sucking on a juice box.The way the entity killed them proved one thing.It wanted to send a clear message to everyone and especially me to what type of powers it had.This thing wanted to instill fear in all of us and wanted us to know it's coming and it's on a warpath.The voice recordings were clear too.On the recordings I could hear this thing say,"Brooks you know what you did and I am coming for you and anyone standing in my way will die with you too."The voice sounded like an old woman.I forwarded the videos and sound recordings to uncle Stephen and he sent it to Yanda for the Senate.

This demonic force is looking for me and it's clear that if I allow it to find me a lot of people will die.I need to go to it or else more innocent people will die.I need to find a way to fight back if I have a fighting chance.I need to go back to the Rocksher farm,maybe I can find something there.I know the twins will assist me.But I also need someone who has been there before.Someone besides the Senate because they will try to stop me.Someone besides Bridget or Sandy or Mr Black or my uncle.Someone who is neutral and won't try to talk me out of going there.One person came to mind.Edmond Yeast.I called Eddie and he agreed to come.He also promised to keep everything a secret.Eddie knew the farm because the Rockshers and Yeast family have always been friends and many of the Yeast family were disciples of the Rocksher cult.As a child he would go to that farm and knows the entrances and exists.Uncle Stephen and everyone that knew about my whereabouts told Karen/Emily that I left the town on work related matters and they had no idea where I went.My car was hidden and the tracker destroyed.She wasn't the person they knew and she was transformed like she was like a wounded animal out for blood according to everyone who saw her.

The following morning I got Edmond and the twins with me and we embarked on our journey to the center of hell.The Rocksher farm.We were armed with things from guns to handgrenades and holy water to crosses and Bibles.We had no idea on what to expect.At Least the twins were part of the Senate and they got trained on how to deal with these things and the Senate was the first to destroy the Rocksher sorcerers before so they would know what to do next.But this time we didn't have an amulet.The amulet used to destroy the Rocksher family the first time just mysteriously disappeared and nobody has an idea of how and who took it.But rumors had it that Clare was the one who stole it again before she left town with her son Thomas.But nobody could prove it was her.

Clare was never seen on the streets when she became mother and nobody even saw her when she left.So it only remained a rumor.The amulet was kept in a secret place on the town premises called the Eye of John.It was a place of prayer and regarded as a holy place.The Senate also created an invisible energy force field by using a spell to keep out any evil.Or any blood relative of the Rocksher family.So if Clare got the amulet she used someone with no blood relationship to the Rockshers or someone within the Senate.Me and my comrades reached the farm and Edmond took is through a pathway on the back of the farmer house.This place was very creepy.It's been overgrown with weeds and tall grass and the Trees haven't been attended to in years.The paint and plastering on the walls started peeling of and the windows were covered in dust.The old stables next to the house had no doors anymore and there was a terrible smell on the place.Eddie led us through a old wooden door next to the stable attached to the old house.This door looked like it was not used a lot because it didn't show signs of friction from being opened and closed.It led us into a staircase that went down into the house and then went upwards again.We got inside a room that had 3 other doors.I turned to Edmond and asked,"Which one?" He looked confused too.On the first door was written,"Sevi Lwa", on the second "Manbo &Oungan",on the third,"Ounsi".I didn't understand what this meant and the Ricky spoke."You see the door that says,Sevi Lwa means the room where they pray to the spirits.Devotional rites are performed here by chanting and dancing into a trance.The one written,Manbo & Oungan are the Priest or Priestess temple.Rituals are performed and knowledge get passed on here from generation to generation.Initiation gets done here too.The third room is written,Ounsi,the congregation room or church church where everyone gets involved in a ritual called the Kanzo.The body becomes the site of spiritual transformation.And possession."I looked at Ricky with amazement at the knowledge the Senate instilled in the members. I felt safer now.So we need to find or out as much as we could in a short space. I asked Ricky which room we should go into and he said there is something we need to find from each room to assist in our quest.Is this guy serious about each room?Now do we have time and the proper experience to pull this off.What if we encounter a force here? Ricky and Johnny took out some strange looking sticks that had a type of crystal at the edge tip and it looked like there was some type of fluid inside the crystal that caused some type of glow at the tip.We entered the Priest room first and I could feel the dark presence in that room.It had two thrones facing each other and there were books and scrolls written in some foreign language.On the altars stood jars full of human organs that made Edmond vomit immediately.The stench was horrible and I covered my nose with a handkerchief I had in my pocket.Johnny picked up the scroll and said if we can read it in this place or open it,it will awaken a darkness in slumber it's better to get it to clean grounds.The scroll had a picture of a snake on it.We went into the second room for prayers and saw grass mats on the floor and Johnny said we shouldn't talk or even sneeze in their because any oral activity will be regarded as activity for worshiping and it will awaken spirits that have been longing for worshipping.Ricky took another scroll that had the picture of a eagle in flight and we went to the last room.The third room was the church room.In this room they had drums and all types of strange musical instruments and there were chalisses for drinking on a altar covered in snake skin.On the walls hang dead snakes and other wild animal carcases all stuffed and dried.Johnny walked over to the altar and took a penny whistle that had blood splattering all over it.The twins knew exactly what we were taking.I told the guys that I needed to check something in the house.I wanted to find something about my grandmother and my father if it was available.The guys were not happy about my idea and wanted us to get out.I got angry and said,"Guys we didn't come here for your trinkets we came here because I asked you to accompany me and now you wanna leave?"They agreed to follow me into the house.We got to the dining area where there were books and pictures laying on the tables.On the walls were pictures of the family.I took out my camera and started taking photos of everything.On the wall was a picture of my grandfather but it had blood on it and below was written in a foreign language.Ricky translated and told me it says."Brooks you know what you did."I got scared and told the guys that we have to go immediately and just as I said that a voice came out of nowhere a very loud and eerie voice saying,"When you awake me from my sleep.At Least stay for a visit."Edmond ran to the door and it shut close.We tried another exit and the doors closed to.The windows got shut and we couldn't get out.The eerie voice started coming closer and said "sit and relax I will entertain you soon."We started banging on the doors and windows but the windows had steel bars and the doors didn't barge at all.Ricky and Johnny started speaking and a foreign language, some type of spell I gathered.This aggravated the spirit even more.The voices grew from one to more than 5 and they started throwing tables and chairs at us.Furniture started hovering above our heads and we ducked and dived for our lives.The twins started waving the sticks around speaking louder in this foreign language that made no sense to me at all and the louder they spoke,the brighter the crystals at the tip of these sticks glowed.And the angrier the spirits became.Ricky have me and Edmond each a necklace made of beads with a crystal at the end just like the ones on their sticks and told us to hang it around our necks.Johnny told us to not show fear because we will give the entities more power as they prey on fear.I started praying even though I have never been in a church my entire life.I just saw a shadow coming straight at me and Johnny pushed me down before it could grab me.It returned again trying to grab a hold of me and I pointed the crystal at it and it screamed and disappeared.I turned around and saw Edmond literally wetting his pants out of fear and I could see a dam of urine forming at his feet.We heard a creepy sound coming from above our heads and when we looked up a monstery figure of a male with long hair and sharp teeth was hovering from the ceiling hanging in an upside down position looking straight at Edmond with eyes like a snake and nails as long as tiger claws.It had feet with razor sharp nails growing from top to bottom, almost looking like roots from an old tree.It licked it's lips and before we could act it swooped down, grabbed Edmond and disappeared into the ceiling.We tried shooting it but it was too late.We could hear Edmond screaming as he was taken away and his screaming sound moved further away from us.We tried chasing after the sound and became silent.The voices came back again and said,"It's only the beginning.We are ready to have fun." We heard a door open and turned around slowly.The door flung open and an object was tossed towards us we moved out of the way in order not to get struck by it and Ricky ran to stop the door from closing but was to late.We looked at the object that was tossed at us and I got sick to my stomach.It was the corpse of Edmond.Sucked dry and crumbled into a ball shape.It didn't even look human anymore.We could only identify Edmond by the clothes.I screamed," come and fight you sick bastards.Don't hide in shadows and come face us."The voice that first spoke to us laughed and said,Oh Brooks my boy we waited on you so long.Welcome back." Ricky told us to brace ourselves for something big is coming.We heard footsteps running in and around and on top of the house from all directions.Johnny took his stick and stuck it in the center of the floor and created a circle around us with some white powdery substance.He gave me silver bullets and told me to load my firearm and shoot at random.He also told me that the circle will hold for a few hours and when night falls it will lose it's power and we have to search into a faith we have never known to win this battle.I asked the twins why we don't use the scroll and artifacts we took from the rooms and use against them? Johnny looked at me and said "The time we took the artifacts the spirits saw.But they didn't have enough power to stop us, they needed to become flesh.They tried to intimidate us and Edmond fell for it and gave them strength through his fear.They consumed his flesh and got stronger but not strong enough.They want us to become tired and scared and give up the fight in order to fuel them up.So these artifacts has power in this house.And if we open them in here it will unleash a greater evil that will give them even more power.If we use these artifacts in here it will turn our hearts wicked and we will fight amongst each other and even kill one another.But outside of here we will have power with these things.All we need do is fight until the sun goes down and come up again in the morning.By then we would have drained their powers and they won't be strong enough to stop us.But if they smell the littlest part of fear they grow stronger." The voices came back and the steps came closer.

Johnny started his language again and Ricky chorused.The doors flung open from all sides and beastly looking creatures with deformities came streaming in and the voice said,"Feed my children".The circle protected us and they stood outside screaming at us and trying their luck at grabbing us while meeting with bullets from our firearms.They are too many and soon we will be running out of ammunition.Rounds upon rounds blazed from our firearms and they kept coming.The eerie voice laughing at us as we fired all around.We continued for hours when we had ran out of bullets and morning sun was 7 hours away.We have been in this house since morning and it's night already.We haven't eaten or drank anything and the legs got weary.And this evil entity knew and observed it while counting the hours.The twins started using manual weapons and gave me a sword too.All weapons made of silver.

I swung away and chopped heads and hands or whatever I could.I looked up at the twins swinging their blades and they looked like real life action heroes and I admired them under all this craziness and for once in my life I felt proud of myself for standing up for myself and the ones I love.For once I was a hero too and I didn't care what the outcome is as long as I know I went out as a man and not a coward.I was happy to have the twins by my side.I could feel the burning in my legs and Ricky saw it too and encouraged me to stay awake and strong by pointing at the corpse of Edmond and whenever he did that I got fire in my soul to go on.Midnight was approaching fast and we had 1 hour left before the circle loses power and we are left exposed and naked to attack.We need a miracle and all the fuel left in our tanks to get through this.We fought and fought and we had 15 minutes left when the voice said,"Tick tock boys.Its gonna be my turn now."Just when he finished saying that we heard gunshots on the outside coming in and the people coming in spoke the same language the twins spoke.I could hear monsters screaming and others running away.Even the evil voices that put us through agony the whole day started running because they knew we had back up and they disappeared into the shadows.It was the Senate.But how did they know we are here?When I looked at the group coming through the door of this demonic house.Guess who was leading the Senate?Yes you guessed correctly.My beautiful wife Karen/ Emily or should I call her Kamily.Yes I think that's a suitable name for her.The combination of both names because I don't know who or what she is.Pastor Shrouder was there and so was Maggie the snake.And many of others I didn't know, some familiar faces that I saw passing in the streets or at Cuppa Jack,but I didn't officially know them.Kamily came over to me and gave me a hug and said,"Honey I was so worried about you I am so glad we arrived in time."How did this lady know I was here.Maggie came forward and said,"Brooks I came to out of the B&B in the morning and I stood on the balcony taking a smoke and I saw you guys crossing through the graveyard towards the lake and when you didn't return I knew something happened and I notified Karen and she called the Senate and we knew that the only place to look for you is the farm house and I am so glad we did."I looked at Maggie and then at Kamily and I could see the guilt in their eyes.What made me more suspicious is the fact that I stood on the balcony several times.What you can see from the balcony is the church, library and the road leading into town and the houses lined up towards the Brooks home.The graveyard is behind the church and you can only see it from the streets because from the B&B balcony the church blocks of the view.Another thing is the lake is further down and maybe if the B&B was build on the library grounds than you would be able to see the lake, because the B&B faces towards the Library and the Library faces towards the lake.The lake can also be seen when you enter the town because the entrance is higher and the town lower.Maggie and Kamily made up this story and they think I am a fool.But I won't make them aware that I am on to them.I just kept quiet and thanked them.We left the farm and took any and everything we needed because now we witnessed the power of this evil and we need to prepare for war.Ricky told me that he was proud of how I became a warrior today and gave me the biggest hug he ever had.Johnny came over and punched me on the arm and said,"It's about high time he stepped up.Good work Peter Parker.You lived up to the Spiderman name.But war is coming Pete we just woke up the dragon and he got a taste of fear."

Chapter 13
Firthlink Cleaner

Uncle Stephen his wife,and his son with his wife and kids stood at the gate holding firearms when we arrived at the Brooks home.Yanda was there,The Blacks and the Yeast and Shrouder family too and many other families that I didn't know.When Bridget looked at me she knew something was wrong she just fell down on the ground and started screaming.The Yeast family started swearing at the Brooks family and said it was our fault that Edmond is dead.My father's half brother even spat me in my face and insulted me.And Ricky put him down with a left and right and he was bleeding from the nose in seconds.The crowd got wild and insults and fist fights started and my great uncle Stephen and his son fired shots to calm everyone down.Great uncle Stephen started speaking standing on top of his SUV."People of the Parish,stop this madness.We are all under danger of this evil that came back.You all know what happened in the past.Our division is only gonna give strength to this demonic spirits and that's what it wants.We need to rally together now for the sake of our children and the future of this town.It's time we stand up as one.Its time we grab our arms and faith and stand up for victory and the ones we lost.Its time we go to War." My great uncle Stephen was very good at motivating people as the crowd started roaring and screaming with a great war cry and I could see in the eyes of the people that they are ready to die for this town.Then I saw another sight.Maggie and Kamily standing far from the crowd and clearly showing on their faces that they are up to some very conniving and they just left without a word or goodbye and nobody noticed but me. My dear wonderful loving wife that's my cousin is walking away after saving my life without a kiss goodnight.I just started laughing and Ricky stopped me because uncle Stephen wanted to talk again.And before Stephen could speak the Yeast family took the body of Edmond and left without wanting any of our help.I felt bad another person died because of trying to help me.Ricky looked at me as I watched the Yeast family load the corpse into the car and said,"Pete my brother this is the casualties of war.Don't be too hard on yourself man."I still couldn't help thinking about his young wife Bridget.She trust me and now her husband is gone.

Stephen stood on his SUV and said,"Friends this is no child's play and people will get hurt and die.So anyone who wants to leave now you are welcome to do that."Nobody wanted to leave and I could see some looked full of doubt and fear but said nothing.Fear of rejection perhaps.Nobody wanted to be known as the one who ran away when the people needed them so they all agreed to stay.Stephen asked his son and daughter in law to pass out a list where everyone can put there names on so that we can have record of everyone in case of death and disappearance.Stephen told them to meet at the Brooks home again tomorrow morning at 7 o'clock for briefing with the Senate and he asked them to bring any silver they had and weapons.I admired these people and how united they stood in the struggle they're about to embark on and the will to stand for something instead of running away.Most of them were wealthy from the mine profits and could move away and leave this war with evil,instead they are willing to fight for what they believe is right.I went to great uncle Stephen when he stepped down from the roof of his SUV and asked him."Uncle Stephen, why don't these people just run away.Why do they wanna risk their lives.He put his hand on my shoulder and said."Bucket my boy.This evil has proven that it can now operate outside of the Parish were it was born and you saw it in Firthlink my boy.Now if it spreads further into the world we won't be safe, no matter where we move to.This is an evil we allowed to live and grow and it's an evil we should stop my boy.The Parish people know that and that drives their will to fight." Wow my great uncle is a very wise man.I never looked at it this way.If we all had this spirit of fighting for something we believed it what a better world will we live in.The crowd dispersed and my uncle Stephen asked the twins to stay over at the Brooks home and they agreed.I felt so happy having my childhood friends with me again and what heroes they are for what they did today in this town that they owe nothing too.Stephen's wife asked us to come and bath and have something to eat. Uncle Stephen took the artifacts from Ricky and put it into his safe.Ricky and Johnny and Stephen put a spell around the house to guard against spirits coming through.They switched on camera and alarms with uncle Stephen's son They were busy outside when Paul shouted,"Hey Pops Mr Marx is at the gate." Mr Edgar Marx is Edmond Yeast's father and I good friend of great uncle Stephen.Edgar came and found us sitting at the dining table eating.Me and the twins.He greeted us all and sat down.Bridget was in his company.He called me and the twins over to where he was seated on the couch and asked us to sit down.He asked for the names of the twins and I introduced Ricky and Johnny.` `My boys I know you feel the pain of losing Edmond today.I know you may blame yourselves for what happened.Here is Eddie's wife next to me and we both came here to tell you it was not your fault and you should finish this war and we need to be strong for the sake of many others standing in the path of destruction from these demonic forces and by the display you put up today we have faith in you.Eddie was a soldier and he died in war so instead of mourning we must celebrate his life.We are all hurting but we must make this evil hurt even more.Lets do it for Eddie and all the others who fell victim to these beasts." Mr Marx grabbed us and gave us a bear group hug and Bridget joined in.

Next morning the Brooks home was filled people all around the yard and in and outside the house.Paul Brooks my uncle and great uncle Stephen's son was busy with Craig Shrouder an old friend of my father and some members of the Senate and they were manufacturing weapons and modifying others.It sparks from grinding and cutting and welding all the way round a hell of a ruckus.Uncle Paul called me over and introduced me Craig and he said the same thing everyone says.``You look like your grandfather William.''I left them and went over to where Pastor Shrouder, Ricky, Johnny, Stephen, Yanda, 4 Senate pastors and Kamily were busy discussing the artifacts we took from the farm.I called uncle Stephen one side.

"What Bucket I am busy my boy?" I looked over at the group and I could see Kamily was looking at me while pretending to be listening to the group,and she saw that I saw she saw me looking at her while looking at me.``Uncle Stephen what is Emily Rocksher doing she here.Yanda told us all to be careful of her and now we are gonna share our secrets with this snake?" Stephen put his hand on my shoulder and said," My boy we are one step ahead of her and we want her close to keep an eye on all her movement.Keep your enemies closer.And don't forget she is actually a Brooks and not a Rocksher so there must be some good in her.Have faith or have a plan.``He turned and walked away from me.This old man had an answer for everything.Kamily wanted to come over to me and I changed direction and walked away quick and fast.She saw it and stopped in her tracks.

My phone rang and it was Fred and he told me that Frankie was next to him.I asked him to put the phone on speaker.``Hey Parker.''I could hear Frankie was very happy to speak to me.``Hey Franklin Dowde how are you brother?"Het giggled like he did when we were growing up."Hey Peter Parker I heard you went from Spiderman to a Ghostbuste?" And he giggled even louder.Frankie loved to tease and joke and he hasn't changed.He could take a serious situation and see the humor in it.Mr Rogers always said,"Dowde are you always the joker.Be serious for once." He always had a joke, Frankie Dowde. Fred stopped Frankie as he wanted to say something silly again. I just heard him say,"And Karen?" Fred spoke before Frankie could say anything else."Pete have you

watched the news since yesterday?"I said things have been crazy here and I told them everything that happened and about my family and Karen.And I asked Fred what's happening on the news."Pete Firthlink is swarming with police, military and the press.The guy Phil Martin.The one that dated Karen was found dead in his apartment just a block away from where you stay.The guy that was missing in action for years was right under our noses.The police found as note that he wanted to send to media telling them about a powerful woman that has him locked in his apartment and he can't go anywhere.And according to media that note has a warning to you Pete saying."Please tell Bucket Brooks he is in danger."The police said the note was found hidden in his refrigerator and the killer never bothered to search there.Phil was stabbed 20 times.Things got worse on the same night, Lisa and Jimmy Colby got burned alive in their home.Nothing was left of their remains.Even the dogs got killed.Mr Rogers and Mr Creddle got attacked the same day and they are both in a coma after the car they were driving was driven off the road.Doctors said they're lucky to still be alive but don't have faith they

will come out of the coma.Only a miracle can save them."I couldn't believe my ears and one name came to my mind Karen.She got information that I was onto her and speaking to these people and she had to kill them because she was afraid they would help me expose her.Only she can be this cruel.I am happy Fred left town just in time."Fred please stay where you are and I will keep you updated.And Frankie please make sure you keep this crazy guy there because he might try to come over and join in on this crazy action.I love you guys and if I never manage to see you again.Just know that I was honored to have friends like you all my life."I dropped the call before they could talk further.

I went back to where Kamily was standing with my uncle Stephen and the Senate.Kamily greeted me and asked for my audience away from the group and uncle Stephen nodded meaning," go ahead and talk to her` `.We stood about 5 meters away from the group and she started talking,"Pete I am sorry about everything I put you through and I just want to fix things between us.I know that we can't be together now that we both found out we are related I know we have to annul our marriage as it's unlawful.Pete my aunt Yanda told me that we are related the time you left town and she told me that she saw you here in the Parish and I came here to tell you everything in person.I didn't want to tell you over the phone.Will you please forgive me Pete I am here to help the town people to beat this evil and get your trust back.Though we can't be lovers because of blood relations I want us to be great as family.Do you forgive me Pete?" I looked at this snake In Front of me and said ,"before I answer your question.Can you tell me why you made me believe you were Karen Grover.And who is Maggie?" She looked me straight in the eye and said Maggie is an old school friend.And I changed my name to get away from my parents who took me to Africa.I wanted to live my dream and be my own person.So I had to change my identity." I had a fire of fury burning inside of me as I looked at this viper spitting out venomous lies.``I forgive you Karen,I mean Emily.We are family after all and family is important." I put my arms around her and gave the most fake hug I ever gave anyone and I hated every moment of it.

Uncle Stephen's words ran through my mind,"keep your enemies close". I asked her if she had a picture of her family and where her brother Stephen was.She told me that she will send me a picture via email and told me Stephen was in Europe on business but will come around here soon.Yanda looked at me as I walked away into the house and I could see she was burning with curiosity.While walking towards the house I told myself that Kamily thinks I am cut of from the world if I am here in the Parish.She thinks I don't know what mess she left behind in Firthlink and she thinks I don't know that Maggie is married to her brother Micheal who is a big gambler and in deep debt.She thinks I don't know that Maggie and Michael are her trackers on me and she promised them shares.She thinks I don't know, that she knew all along that she is a Brooks and got married to me knowing very well.She did all this to get close to me and everyone I love to fulfill her evil plan whatever it is.But I will find out why and what and cut the head of the dragon.Why does she want to help us.What is she gonna gain from it. It's clear she has a vendetta.She is more Rocksher than Brooks and I can't believe I shared a bed for years with this demonic force.I went straight to the kitchen and got myself a cold beer and downed it with one vicious blow and got another one and did the same.The third I took and walked towards the sitting room.

Yanda was standing in the kitchen looking at me the whole time and I only saw her when I turned around.``Bucket I know you are angry,but drinking yourself to death is not a solution my boy.We still need you and I believe we will win this thing." I was becoming a very angry person and the lovely Bucket was becoming a Bucket full of anger.``My boy anger will turn your heart full of hate.And before you know it Bucket you will become as evil as the evil you trying to destroy.Don't lose yourself in the process of fighting your problems.You shouldn't turn your heart into a prison of old bones and curses my boy.Stay who you are before you lose what you should become,and stop getting drunk it's not my birthday yet.By the way what did Emily want?"I told Yanda everything and she told me that Emily never spoke to her in years until yesterday and she should not be trusted."Bucket just don't buy into her lies and keep playing along.A snake can lay in the grass but I will always lift its head to strike.Be awake and don't slumber or sleep.Steady yourself for when it's time to strike a killer blow to that snake's head.``At Least I know Yanda is on my side.``Aunty Yanda,why didn't my grandmother ever reach out to me or my father?" She just shook her head and I knew she had no idea why.Yanda took the beer out of my hand and said," Go take a little nap.I will come check up on you later.Just relax.``Aunt before you go, where is Emily's brother Michael?"She smiled and said,"He is in Firthlink my boy.

He was close to you all the time and you didn't know.``I had to ask again.``Yanda, how did Emily know I was at the Rocksher farm because the story Maggie made up has no sense?" Yanda paused and said, "Did Emily ever give you presents?"I said yes and showed her the watch I had to n was one of the gifts.Yanda just looked at me once and said,"There is your answer the watch has a tracker you can bet on it.Go rest and stop all the questions before you go mad." I took a blanket from Paul's bedroom and lay down on the couch.I fell asleep so fast, must be the beer and fatigue.I went into a dream.In my dream I found myself walking through the graveyard and as I strolled in the graveyard a huge snake appeared In Front of me.The stood facing me and I looked it square in the eyes.It turned around and started digging up corpses and eating them.The corpses screamed as the snake devoured them one by one.And then a girl dressed in red clothes appeared and started feeding the snake human organs from a bucket and the snake stopped eating corpses and lay flat on it's stomach like a dog when it's happy and lifted it's head slightly so the girl could drop the organs in it's mouth.The girl turned the bucket upside down showing the snake the organs are finished and the snake got sad and she turned towards me and her eyes turned into snake eyes too and she pulled me towards her with a magnetic force and I could move.Her nails started growing long into shapes of knives and she lifted me up in the air by using her eyes and dropped me hard on the graveyard soil.The snake was watching and waiting on the girl to remove my organs and just as she was about to strike her long nails into my flesh Yanda woke me up.I was soaked wet from sweating.Yanda told me that I was jerking in my sleep and she has been trying to wake me up for a whole 30 minutes and when I looked my uncle and the twins were there with Yanda.I told them my dream and Johnny told me they had to cast a spell over me to wake up.Pastor Shrouder was also there and he told me I was almost taken by spirits in sleep.They would've killed me or taken my soul to the darkness and to get my soul back would be difficult because someone has to enter the demon world to save another and many don't make it back.

I couldn't believe what almost happened to me.I dripped from head to toe,sweat running down my body.Yanda told me to sit up straight and she gave me this dark smelly fluid from a silver canasester.It tasted horrible.Yanda said it will help me feel the presence of evil spirits when I am asleep and assist me to wake up easily.Johnny gave me a ring with a red crystal and told me to wear it on my left hand index finger.I asked why I am the only one with a ring and Pastor Shrouder told me because they only have one and at this point I need it more as the prime target.It made sense.I took of my watch and gave it to Paul.I asked him to check if it had a tracker and if it did he shouldn't take it out because I want to use it as a trap.Yanda looked at me and said,"You still want to wear it again?"Yanda and everyone don't understand that by keeping this watch and making Karen believe that I have no idea about the tracker in my watch,will enable me to use it to my advantage.Lets say for argument sake I get abducted then my family can track me and without her knowing we have knowledge of the tracker gives us the upper hand.I got up from the couch and the noises outside were still heavy.Ricky told me that the people made a lot of weapons and bullets from silver they melted down.We walked outside and saw a car coming in.I looked over to Paul and asked,"Who are those people coming in at the gate?"He punched me lightly on the arm and said," You ask them yourself." The strangers came closer and then I remembered who they were.I remember Mr Rogers showing me pictures of the Rocksher family and I couldn't remember were I saw the pictures.Its the same people in the picture I saw and it the same picture I saw Karen putting into her purse and when I asked her she didn't want to show me.Now I remember and now I know why.It's her parents Thomas and Deena and her sister Lora.She knew I would find out the truth that's why she hid the pictures.They came over to me and before they could say anything I just grabbed my father's twin brother and held him tight while bawling my eyes out.Tears just streamed from my eyes and he held me too and we both just cried.I didn't have to say anything because he already knew who I was and vise versa.

Chapter 14
Homecoming

It's Saturday morning and the day the Annual dance was supposed to take place but it has been canceled because we are preparing for a war.The town has been sealed off for anyone coming or going.A force field has been created right around the town to keep all demons within the boundaries of the Parish. We have all committed to this cause and we will die for it.Last night I sat with my father's twin brother and his wife and my cousin Lora and her son Xavier who is 12 years old now.We spoke about my life and everything they needed to know about my upbringing.And then I asked about my grandmother, Clare.Uncle Thomas was busy stuffing his tobacco pipe just like my father used to do.It was like looking at my father.They were so similar and looked identical."Bucket my son." I felt so warm inside when he called me son.Not Brooks, Pete, Parker, Bucket or Peter,but son.I felt like my father was back again.Mr Black,Sandy and Mrs Black were there too because Mr Black wanted to see the man that looks like his childhood friend.Mr Black couldn't stop staring at Thomas and I could see him get a little irritated with my uncle Thomas when he called me son.I think Mr Black felt that I was the son he wanted and he got Preston back,by having me here and I could just imagine what he was thinking,"Who is this guy calling Brooks his son.He wants to steal my boy away?" Uncle Thomas started telling me things that made my skin crawl."Bucket, did you ever ask your great aunt Yanda the whole reason why my grandfather Thandai left this town?"I said,"no."Well my son.I am gonna share things with you that I believe you need to know.Thandai was a good person and a man of peace just like your sweet aunt Yanda and it's so strange to grasp the fact that they were born from such evil.When Clare got involved with William Thandai and his wife knew and threw a blind Thandai believed that getting some good blood

121

in the family like the Brooks blood might be something positive for the future generations of Rocksher offspring.He and his wife tried everything to keep the relationship a secret from the Rockshers but because they are so evil they managed to find out.Well Clare got summoned to the farm for her indiscretions and she had to come up with a plan to through them offline.Now people were dying left right and center on the Parish grounds and when the town needed someone to help them destroy the Rockshers, Clare put up her hand.Because the Rockshers wanted to destroy Clare's relationship,she knew that she had to destroy them first and the only way to do that was to join them.To destroy your enemies you have to get into their camp.Clare was thought everything about sorcery because her grandmother believed she wanted to be part of them and destroy the Brooks and everyone who went against them.And I am sure you know everything thing else my mother Clare did to destroy the Rockshers."

Uncle Thomas took a puff from his tobacco pipe and started speaking again."Well with the Rocksher family destroyed and Clare pregnant the town seemed more peaceful.We could walk around at night again and we felt safe.Now remember the sorcerer's had many disciples and they wanted revenge and things turned sour very soon and fast.Other disciples wanted to promote themselves to Priesthood and worked even harder to activate demonic spirits again that would bring terror back and they succeeded for a short period and many people died again.In that short period my grandfather Thandai became a bigger target and he had no choice but to take his kids and run.Rumors went around that Thandai was ashamed of his teenage daughter but that wasn't true.Well Clare got touched by spending time at the farm and she was transforming into her grandmother.She would speak strange things and her taste in cuisine changed.At first they thought it was her pregnant state but clearly something else was happening to her.And when William went on and married the Yeast lady she snapped and became evilness itself.She was found strangling cats and playing with snakes and spiders.Thandai knew that this town was bad and had to run with his family.The day before they had to leave Clare went into labor and they had to delay the William wanted to take both kids from Clare and the Rockshers and Brooks had a fight and it was agreed that the boys be split.I went with my mother Clare and Preston stayed here.I grew up knowing about my family the Brooks family but I was forbidden to make any contact with them or come to this town for the fear of bringing evil with me.The day Preston was taken away from my mother she cursed William and told him she will haunt him all his life.The morning Thandai and his family left town Clare ran away to Europe and that's why aunt Yanda went there to look for her not because of her own will but to search for Clare.Thandai waited for 5 weeks until Yanda told him to leave the Parish because she can't find Clare and she might be in Europe a bit longer.Yanda took 14 months and found Clare in a village in France living amongst Haitian people.Yanda didn't have to ask what she was doing there because the group was into voodoo and sorcery and it was clear that the allegations were true that Clare has moved over to darkness.Yanda had to do some pleading and praying to get her on a plane again with me as a toddler.They say love conquers all and she agreed to come back with Yanda but only if she can stay in the Parish with Yanda.Time passed until she decided to make up a lie and move to Firthlink with me.I am sure my mother Clare planned all this and I won't put it passed her.Why did she go back to her father's house."

Sandy was gauging at my uncle Thomas as he spoke."Well my mother didn't take care of me anymore when we moved to Firthlink and she was always in her room during the day and would walk around the yard at night.She would chant and speak in foreign languages that I couldn't understand.My grandparents were afraid of her as if she put a spell on them.Even the house staff were afraid of her and didn't even clean or go into her room.I remember when an employee went into her room once just to sneak,he saw something that he wasn't supposed to see and ran away never to be seen ever again.

Clare would stand at the window and watch people pass by but she would never go out on the streets or maybe she did when nobody saw at night.My mother Clare's homecoming was not a very welcoming one for my grandparents and they showed in the way they feared her and agreed to everything she said.She had her spell working on them.I became and adult and I got married and had kids.My grandparents passed away and she never went to the funeral.But people said they saw her at the graveyard at night sitting next to her parents graves.Come to think my mother Clare wasn't even at my graduation or wedding.I never had a relationship with my mother and even as an adult I could see how she would look at me with loveless eyes, but it never bothered me because I received a lot of love from my grandparents and I never thought of Clare as my mother.The one thing that I couldn't understand is the fact that she loved my kids and spend all her time with them in her room.And she would play with them in the house when the house staff wasn't around and eventually got me to lay off all the staff members because she felt that she didn't have enough freedom with her grandkids.I saw it as something positive and believed my other had changed.She would do the cooking and cleaning herself and she kept the house very neat.The kids were happy and me and my wife appreciated everything she was doing.Things went well for years until Lora came to me one day and said,"Daddy ,I want to go to boarding school. I don't want to stay in this house anymore."This was very strange to me.I thought they enjoyed spending time with their grandmother.I called the other two over and they told me that they enjoyed everything they did with their grandmother.I believed that Lora was just being selfish or going through adolescence.Either way I didn't get my daughter to have her way.Lora started coming home late and a lot of times she would take the bus to my office or her mother's workplace just to be away from the house.I started becoming suspicious of my mother and started zooming in on her activities with my children.I would see Micheal and Emily go into her room daily.They would spend hours in there but Lora wasn't interested.Lora came back to me and her mother about the boarding school idea and we shut it down again until she decided to run away from home.We searched for a whole week until we found her staying with the Creddle family and we never thought she would go there because we didn't really have a close relationship with the Creddles.Mr Creddle had a young daughter Tammy and she and Lora were in the same class.Lora told Tammy that she was scared to be at home and her friend helped by hiding her.I spoke to Lora and she told me about the voodoo dolls and the spells and chanting their grandmother made them partake in.She also told me that spirits lived in the house, and they spoke to their grandmother and to Michael and Emily, and she got afraid to take part.Her grandmother told her if she could tell anyone outside the house she would send the spirits to kill her and she never told anyone but me. I send Lora to boarding school and my mother Clare wasn't even concerned.Instead she was always happy around Micheal and Emily and vise versa.She never asked about Lora and even when Lora came back from school break she didn't even look in her direction or show affection or attention towards her.It was evidently clear to me that she found two disciples and she was happy with their progress.I approached my mother and she just looked at me once and walked away.I saw by the look in her eyes that I made a grave mistake.I received a call the following day from Lora's boarding school and they told me Lora was gravely ill and she was admitted to hospital.The doctors tried everything and my child's health just deteriorated.Months went by and nothing changed.I came back from the hospital one evening and my mother walked up to me,gave me a bottle with medicine and said,"Make Lora drink this."I was scared but what was my chances and I did as she said.I left the hospital and before I could start my car they called me back and said Lora woke up.I took my child home same day and my mother just smiled at us and said,"I know everything and have the power over everything and she disappeared into her room.I was more terrified of her and didn't bother her and the two disciples for fear of our lives.My wife and I noticed how Michael and Emily withdrew from social society and spend more and more time with my mother.I would get complaints from school on they would give other children bleeding noses and how kids were found bound up in restrooms with strange words and languages written on their foreheads.This one time they even went to the graveyard with the neighbors dog and mutilated it.The security guard working at the graveyard witnessed it and when he was asked to testify he suddenly fell ill and started getting blisters and sores all over his body even on his privates and in his mouth.And a week later he was miraculously healed and he resigned from work, left town and never came back again." Thomas took another puff from his pipe and said.

"How we ended up in Africa is another story.I started doing my own research and a friend from Kongo told me that every cult following has a monarchy and they are all protected by a amulet.The amulet,if placed in the hands of a pure hearted person reverse power and the evil can be destroyed by that amulet and even killed.Now I didn't want to kill my other and my children.I just wanted to destroy their powers.Than I remembered in Levensdown Parish they used the amulet of Tomoko Rocksher to capture and destroy them.I called Yanda and she told me that the amulet was stolen from the town and nobody had any idea of who took it and where it could be.My Kongolese friend told me if I can't find the amulet I need to go back to the temple of the disciples origin and get three artifacts that I will use to break their powers.The second option is to go back to the origin of the high Priest or Priestess and get the village Mallam to create a spell for me to destroy this evil.So going back to Levensdown Parish was not an option I wasn't gonna risk coming back here and go on that farm where evilness lay dormant and can be activated by my presence,so I decided on Africa.I spoke to Michael and I knew he had a bit of a loose tongue and I asked him how this sorcery worked, making him believe I wanted to join the family trait.He fell for it hook line and sinker and knowing my boy to be a bit of a braggart he sang all types of tunes trying to prove to me how advanced and far his powers were.I learned that as long as the disciples from a group can hold onto their amulet nobody can break their powers,and nobody can touch them.Now that the amulet has disappeared Africa was our only option.I asked Michael if you go to the place where the high Priest of their congregation originate from what can you achieve in terms of power?Michael being himself told me that you can do that if you want to become a high Priest and gain more power.But he also told me being close to the place of origin can be dangerous as the Mallam from that village can kill you to steal your powers or he can just steal your powers and leave you useless.I asked Mike if I wanted to become a high Priest will I be able to and he said he would ask his grandmother and he did.She called me to her room for the first time since she came here with me as a child.

My mother smiled at me for the first time in years and she said."This is really a homecoming.Please join me my son",as she pointed at a grass mat on the floor indicating that I should sit there."Tommy my grandson tells me you want to be part of this great legacy your ancestors have practiced for generations and I feel so happy knowing our heritage continues.Now Tommy since your a pure soul and don't know how things work and have never used dark magic I believe that you will be the perfect candidate for high Priest.The Mallams from those villagers won't have power over you because you are pure and they can't steal anything from you.You will have to go through the initiation by being trained by another high Priest and I can't do that because I am still lowly to train a high Priest.This is a very jovial occasion for me my son."I looked around the creepy room filled with dead creepy crawlers and scrolls and jars.When did she bring all these things in here without us noticing."So when are we going Tommy because I need to prepare everything and ask the spirits to guide me to the right person to help you when we get to the homelands."I said we need to sort out our Visa's first and we will go.She was very excited and singing this strange song.I asked her can Micheal and Emily become a high Priest and Priestess too.? "She smiled and said,"Yes they can after years,but they won't be as strong as you because you're going into this as a pure soul and they're already tainted by darkness."I got out of that room before she started offering me creepy crawlers to eat."

"My plan was coming together but I didn't allow my mother or her disciples to know what my real motive was, especially Emily she has always been conniving and observant.Nothing could pass her by she was always investigating and planning.A real snake.I am sorry to say that about my child but she is.Didn't you become suspicious when none of her family came to your wedding and you never met a single member.The house you own in Firthlink was a gift from my grandparents to Emily before they died and when you thought you were buying a house you didn't know you were buying from her, your wife.She played you from day one and she knew who you were we just need to find out how you fit into whatever she's planning and it revolves around you Bucket.We had our Visa's made and everything was arranged.We left Firthlink at night without anyone noticing.My mother was over the moon.My Kongolese friend arranged at place to stay and he had to only assist me in finding the right Mallam to assist with my matter regarding these 3 evil beings.We blended in with the community,I got the kids into a school in the city and I bought shares in a mining company and sat on the board of directors overseeing the business development division.My wife took a job as a teacher and we looked like a normal family and nobody knew the evil that lurked behind the walls of my home.It didn't take long before Michael and Emily started their old tricks. Children and teachers started complaining about them.I spoke to my mother and she reprimanded them.She told them that things are different in Africa and soon they might find themselves facing other's stronger than them,and they did.My mother started disappearing at night and I would only hear her voice in the bedroom in the morning.I would never see her when she leaves or when she comes back.I suspected that she was up to her old traits again.People suddenly disappeared in the community and others were found with organs missing.My Kongolese friend told me that he knows of a group of sorcerers about 5 km from where I stayed.I had to find this place and track my mother when she leaves at night.I did and I found that she had become part of the group.The second time I tracked after he she caught me.She was furious and I told her that I tracked her because I was in a hurry to become high Priest.She believed my story and told me that I shouldn't be approaching these people myself because I know nothing about sorcery and they might use me in sacrificial rituals.She promised to get me connected to the right people and told me that her night trips was regarding this, but I didn't believe everything she told me."Everyone, including me, was just quiet while listening to uncle Thomas.I studied his pipe and shook his head slowly and I could see he was very sad.And he spoke again.

"Yes Bucket my son it was gonna get worse before it got better.I was doing the same thing my mother did to her family years ago when she betrayed them because they were evil and she was in love.I could see mother changing everyday even her facial appearance wasn't the same anymore.Her eyes were red and her nails grew longer than normal.She didn't even wear shoes anymore.About a 5 years went by and she hadn't spoken about me becoming a high Priest.I believed she was busy becoming a high priestess herself and didn't trust me.I contacted my Kongolese friend and he arranged for me to meet a Mallam which was risky for all of us but I had to try.The meeting was arranged and the Mallam told me what he needed for this ritual and I had to get them all otherwise the ritual won't work.He needed personal artifacts from Michael, Emily and my mother he provided me with the list of everything.On the day he had to perform the ritual my Kongo friend called me the Mallam was found dead with his eyes and tongue pulled out.He was too weak for my mother who was getting stronger.The artifacts he had to use was gone.I was back at square one.A month went by again and I didn't ask my mother anything and I could see by the way she looked at that she knew I was the one who took the artifacts from the house and given it to the Mallam.She didn't say it but I saw it in her eyes and the fact that Michael and Emily kept distancing themselves from me.They only tolerated me because I am family but I need to watch my moves.

My Kongo friend came to visit me.He asked me to go out to the village with him.I took my car keys and we took my car.We went to a house with high walls and solid steel gates.He told me press the hooter and someone came to the gate and opened it for us.I drove and parked on the side of the house.The person that opened the gate told us to follow him inside.An old man sitting on a throne welcomed us and told us to sit.I could see by the way he was dressed that he was a powerful man.His amulets showed that he was highly ranked.He said to the servant to fetch his grandson.A chubby boy with a hand full of candy and a piece of cake in the other,about 16 years of age ,standing In Front of us.The old powerful man on the throne introduced himself as Mallam Bungari and his chubby cake devouring grandson Zengala.Mallam Bungari said," Zangala stop chewing before you explode."The boy swallowed so fast almost choked."Tell Mr Rocksher what you told me." The boy hesitated and Mallam said,"Talk boy we haven't got all day." He came closer to me and said," Mr Rocksher I attended the same school with your children.Now I was afraid to talk until I told my grandfather.Micheal and Emily threatened to kill me if I said a word.They made me eat spiders and rats and nasty things and they would use spells to make me lift up from the ground and hover for periods between 10-30 minutes and drop me down with just a wave of their hands.I have never seen so much power and I was very scared.My grandfather saw me vomiting outside and I had to tell him everything." I looked at the Chubby boy who kept stuffing his face in between talking to us and I almost said,"They wanted to get you to lose weight."Mallam Bungari got up from his throne and said,"Mr Rocksher I know that you are not into the practice of dark magic and you actually brought your family here to break the spirit possession they're under.I know Mr Rocksher your friend Pandu told me.Mr Rocksher I can understand by the power your children possess means the one who trained them is even more powerful and I am sure I will need help in this regard.They might be too strong for me.But don't worry Mr Rocksher your friend brought you to the right place.

Chapter 15
Mallam Bungari

Yanda asked us if anyone wanted something to drink and went into the kitchen.The noise outside the Brooks home started to subside as the crowd slowly started going home.They were waiting on the Senate for a go ahead on when to strike the farm and anyone involved with the Rocksher cult following.A list was already drafted with suspects that were disciples and practicing darkness.Some had already skipped town when news came in that the Senate had arrived and those that are still here are trapped within the boundaries of this Parish.Yanda came back from the kitchen with drinks and snacks and placed it in the table in front of us.Sandy called me outside and said I should keep her company while she smoked.Uncle Thomas said,"Go join Sandy Bucket I want to fill my pipe to.Outside the weapons were taken to the secret room underneath Stephen's garage and other members of the Senate were briefing members on the next step.Sandy put her arm around my waist and said," We miss you at the B&B and my parents can't stop talking about you." I felt the same.The Blacks have become family to me.``I saw Emily/Karen or whatever her name is earlier when she left here with Maggie." I giggled and said,"I call her Kamily now." Sandy cracked with laughter.We went back in and I had some coffee.Uncle Thomas started talking again.``Yes Bucket as I was saying.The Mallam Bungari told me to give him contact numbers and he will call me when everything was arranged.I begged him not to kill my family.I only wanted their powers to be destroyed.Mallam Bungari agreed and me and Pandu left.A whole 2 months went passed and nothing.The town became a haven of evil and it was evidently clear that my mother and her new made friends was behind all this.I lived in constant fear and so did my wife and Laura.Eventually the Mallam called and asked for my audience.I told him that my mother had already killed another Mallam and he told me that he knew.Mallam Bungari had 10 other Mallams with him making them 11 in total and they also got the community alerted of what was about to transpire.They had formulated their own potions and spells and I had no idea what they're doing.They found my mother and her congregation busy with a ritual and the body of a pastor that disappeared a week ago was on the altar and getting stripped from internal organs.They were caught off guard and captured after long hours of spell wars and physical encounters.Blood and skin flying all-round as they battled for hours until eventually they got overpowered and captured.They were all burned at the stake while I watched.My own mother killed in front of my eyes and I couldn't do anything.I was completely helpless,Bucket.That night I cried non stop.Michael and Emily knew what had happened the town wasn't that big and almost everyone knew anyone.The community allowed me to bury my mother's ashes and it was very emotional for me.I started regretting my decision to come here and felt that my children are exposed to the same fate now that Mallam Bungari know they're my mother's disciples.I called Mallam Bungari after my mother's burial and asked him why he didn't stick to our original agreement and instead of telling me why,he just asked about the whereabouts of Michael and Emily and I knew that we had to run from this town.And going back home was not an option because Firthlink and Levensdown were absolutely no go zones so I had to find another place.I knew Mallam Bungari wasn't gonna let my children survive and the possibility that my whole family could be eliminated was very high,so running was the best option.We took what we could could and made it to the nearest boarded and took a flight to the Libanese region where we still live today.Emily and Michael started behaving well and we started living as a normal family and the past started fading away.I changed my contacts and broke all connections with my Kongo friend Pandu because I didn't trust him anymore and I was correct.A few months later I found a newspaper article about him being arrested for dealing in human organs.I was relieved knowing we escaped from him.All three of my children finished school and went to University but Emily decided to come here and study here and I never saw her ever again until now.Years and years passed and the fact that she changed he names made it difficult to trace Mallam Bungari wanted my mother's powers and I am sure he and his goons are very strong now and Pandu was the one who recruited us into the Dragon's mouth."My uncle Thomas gave out a sigh,I didn't know if it was relief or pain."Yes, Bucket now you know my son.I need to get going I promised Yanda here.(Pointing at her), that I will be having dinner with her at the Owl." He got up and bid us all a good day and they left with Yanda.

I looked at the twins and asked them."Guys if this thing was destroyed here and in Africa but it still keeps coming back,why?"Before the twins answered, Pastor Shrouder said,"The Rocksher amulet."My uncle Stephen got up and said,"Yes Shrouder is correct, the amulet is still operating somewhere out there and giving power to the spirits.Even if we keep striking a killer blow at the dragon another head will grow because of this amulet.Like the Mallam Bungari.He took the powers of Clare and is stronger now and while the amulet is still out there he will become stronger and if can get it he will have powers beyond control and can even come and rule over us here.Our only hope will be to find that cursed thing."Ricky and Johnny agreed with my uncle Stephen.

Everyone had left the Brooks yard and uncle Stephen's son Paul came back with my watch."Bucket your watch does have a tracker but now I have inserted another chip so I can be able to track your movement too.And the people are all gone outside and everything is packed and ready for us to go to war." Uncle Stephen's wife stood up and said guys I think we need to set up a trap for these demonic forces and the disciples.I think we still have time for the Annual Dance.We already made all the preparations and I think the dance will be a way to pull them out.My great aunt had a point.She looked at Paul and said,"Boy,start sending out messages to the people,tell them the dance is on." I saw the Blacks looking over at me and smiled.They got their wish now I had to take Sandy to the dance.Within an hour the Senate was at the Brooks home.Weapons got loaded onto cars and moved to the dance hall were it would be hidden on the premises making sure everything happened.Mr Black took me on the shopping trip he promised.We didn't have enough time so everything was done hush hush.I got a black tuxedo and black shoes and Mr Black forced me to get haircut and shave.Night came and the whole town's people gathered at the dance hall.I went to the B&B and picket Sandy up.Strange thing happened when we got to the dance hall and Kamily was there waiting at the entrance.She walked up to me and said,"Hey honey I thought you were gonna come pick me up for the dance?"I just walked past her with Sandy on my arm, without saying a word.She tried to grab my arm and I pulled away.Karen was really sick.She still calls me honey knowing full well that we are related.How sick can someone be.

Chapter 16
The Dance

The DJ spoke over the microphone."Peach Town,can we have a moment of silence for our friend Edmond Yeast who has fallen in war.And to those before him." Then he spoke again and said,"This year we will ask Bucket Brooks and Sandy Black to open up the floor for us.Sandy and Bucket on the floor please.I wasn't scared because if there was one thing I knew was dancing.I was the one who always worked out the choreography for the Blue Boys when we still tried being a boy band.Karen and I would dance for hours and I thought her everything about dancing.I looked over to where Karen was standing and I could see the green monster in her eyes.I grabbed Sandy by the waist and took her one hand into mine.We swirled around and then as if Sandy knew exactly what moves to make we rattled up the crowd and soon the dance floor was full of moving bodies.We had great fun into the night.Refreshments were available and I took Sandy to the table where it was served and poured us some champagne.Kamily came over and asked me where her drink was.I couldn't take this anymore and had to open my mouth."Karen or whatever your name is, can you please understand that we are blood relatives and we can never ever be together again.And Sandy and I are not in s relationship and even if we were, that's not your concern so please stop harassing me."She gave me a real evil look and walked away.I thought for a second she was gonna take a knife and slit my throat.The whole evening we kept our distance away from Karen.

Almost everyone in the town was there.We had a jovial time. I even saw Yanda getting her bougie down.But I also noticed that my uncle Isaac who is part of the Yeast family was not there and with all the Yeast family.Sandy told me that a lot of other town people were not there and I could understand why.We danced until 2 in the morning.Until Ricky came in and took the microphone from the DJ and started speaking."People I just came back from the Brooks home and as I came here I witnessed someone standing outside the gate of the Dance Hall.I walked up to him and asked why he was outside and everyone inside.He turned around and this person had a eyes as big as golf balls that was hollowed out.He had razor sharp teeth and he was half snake and half human.He came for me and I am stabbed it twice with my silver sword.He came back again and I started using spells against it.And it vanished towards the Rocksher farm.I think we should get ready they are coming."

Pastor Shrouder told everyone who could fight to follow him and Paul and Johnny and other members of the Senate to where they hid weapons.Every abled body person was given a weapon and a post.Force fields got created around kids and those that couldn't fight to protect them against attacks.Karen called the Senate to the center of the floor and asked me and the twins to take out the artifacts we stole from the Rocksher farm.She took out some strange looking canister and poured out some powdery substance that looked like human ashes onto the artifacts.And she asked the Senate to start casting trap spells onto the artifacts while we placed our hands on them.As the trap spells were chanted the artifacts started creating a glow and melted together and combined into big amulet.Karen asked Pastor Shrouder to hang it around his neck and make sure he stays within the circle and he must not stop chanting.She then told us to put out our hands as she poured some smelly red coloured oil over everyone's hands that was armed to fight.This oil smelled horrible.The twins told me to stay close to them and brace myself for anything that could come through the doors.I looked at Karen and didn't even ask how she knew what to do and how.I just looked at her and said to myself,"She's a wicked witch it's obvious she will know these things."We were here ready to fight waiting on whatever was coming through these doors or windows when suddenly there was a knock on the door and someone was screaming hysterically.Ricky peeped through the window and said," it's an old man and he looks scared." Craig Shrouder went to the window and said,"It's Gavin Right, the village drunk, open for him." Just as we opened the door to let Gavin in I saw big claws coming from above the Dance Hall sweep down and swept Gavin away,same as happened to Edmond and before we could close the door shadows flew in and started taking the scared and weak within seconds before we could react.Karen started screaming," don't show fear they can smell it and wants to feed in order to become flesh.They smell your fear."The Senate screamed,"Close the doors and before we could close the doors 5 people were taken,6 including Gavin."They're coming back", Karen said and told the Senate to put the vulnerable into a room and she cast a spell to protect the room and she said," we must work fast when they get back because our protective shields will hold only for some time."

Running footsteps came towards the Hall from all angles and soon these demonic forces broke into the hall and war began.I looked over and saw everyone fighting and slaying with all their powers,but Karen was just moving around and a circle and these things didn't even attack her as if she was the puppet master pushing them in all directions.One beast made an attempt to attack her and she just pointed her fingers at it and it fled away from her getting slaughter by a swinging blade from Pastor Shrouder.Some of these beasts tried moving towards the room we placed the vulnerable and in front of the room growling and getting angry because they couldn't get in the room because of the protective shield.Karen pointed at her watch which meant that we are running out of time.She moved to the center of the ring where Pastor Shrouder and she grabbed his right hand and started chanting something that I have never heard before.She and Pastor Shrouder lifted up in the air as if being zoomed up by aliens and hovered,her eyes started glowing and her hair stood up straight.Pastor Shrouder started jerking like a car with a short distribution flow and his eyes started glowing too, a bright red glow and he started speaking this strange language too as if

Karen was transferring her powers to him.Then the two of them started pointing at the center of the floor where the circle was drawn and a light started radiating from the amulet on Pastor Shrouder's neck and created a blue flame coming through the floor,that started devouring these beasts and they tried running but nothing could save them.Karen and the Pastor floated towards the doors and floated out into the yard that was creeping with these these things.The Senate and all of us that could fight followed Karen and the Pastor while firing left right center.The blue flames devoured them and our bullets worked as well. As we fought I asked myself where Karen was at the Rocksher farm.Her skills are making this war a breeze and we don't have many casualties.We destroyed every single entity.At the Dance Hall and on the streets and we saw others moving towards the Rocksher farm where we chased them to.We are going back to the belly of the beast.Karen and the Pastor came down from their hovering and floating and touched the ground.They were still glowing and still chanting in this foreign language while walking ahead of us.When we got to the farm gate the amulet around Pastor Shrouder's neck starting acting weird as it was trying to indicate that evil was laden heavy on these planes,it was swinging and jumping up and down around the Pastors neck.As soon as we stepped onto the premises the earth started vibrating as if a earthquake was coming.I looked at the group and saw that some were getting scared and I even smacked one standing next to me and I screamed,"No fear warriors,for today we lay the beast." I saw my words giving them courage as they rushed towards the house kicking and slamming doors down.Firearms rang on the inside and I enjoyed the sound of demonic forces screaming and fleeing.The earth vibrated heavier and split open.Something was coming through the ground and I just heard the screaming of a group of 6 men behind me.As I turned I saw what was clearly the tail of a giant snake.The snake grabbed the 6 men by it's tail and crushed them with one blow.It came back and grabbed more and more men and women.And then the ground split further and it's head came up standing 10 meters above us just as it was about to strike me down.Karen pulled out another amulet from her pockets and pointed it at this snake.Bullets rang inside and around the house as beasts got slayed and here we stood facing the giant snake that was rumored for years.As Karen pointed the amulet the snake it wanted to crawl back into the ground,but Karen wouldn't allow it.She stood eye to eye with it and started chanting something else.Pastor Shrouder still in his trans followed suite and chanted the same words as if it was rehearsed.The snake could not move and looked like it was caught in a choke lock.Then with a deep demonic voice Karen screamed to at me,"Bucket Brooks take it down now.Strike it,cut it's head off immediately Brooks.I looked at Snake grabbed a sword from Johnny and without any hesitation I cut its head off with one heavy blow and it dropped to the ground with a thud and dust flew up as it hit the surface.Karen then spoke few more words and all the demons started fading away.Pastor Shrouder and Karen got out of the trans and a great roar of victory found its way around the grounds of the farm and could be heard cities away.Hugs and tears went all around and I even found myself hugging Karen and thanking her for helping us.Karen went over to where to the house and said,"Burn it down now."And that's exactly what we did.We burned down every inch of that farm and left nothing untouched,even the secret rooms and chambers.It was a great victory for the town of Levensdown Parish and I could see the relief in the eyes of everyone.

Chapter 17
Yesterday

A month went by after our victory and it was another Saturday again.Disciples that worked for the Rocksher family were caught and burned,and those like my uncle Isaac and the other Yeast family who ran away were left to be found another day.They can't run forever.It was a happy atmosphere and everyone wanted to just dance and be happy.Pastor Shrouder who was also the Mayor decided to put up a memorial site for the fallen heroes and also for the ones that fought with bravery against an evil that became a tyrant to this community and outside like places like Firthlink.Pastor Shrouder that a commemoration day and medals of bravery will be handed out to everyone who was involved and it is planned for a month from now,for people involved directly or indirectly.It will be a posh event and Sandy asked me for a second date.A proper one with no guns and snakes.I agreed and even Karen gave us her blessings.Karen and I put our bad blood aside and accepted the fact that we are family and need to stick together.Smiles were on the faces of everyone, even the ones that lost family members.Food tasted better and even the wind blew with a whistling melody.It was like a magic wand was waved over this land and all bad things went away.Maggie just disappeared and nobody knows how and when she left town.I asked Karen and she didn't know too.I didn't delve much into it because Karen was a hero in these parts now and I had faith in her again after a long time.Sandy and I started getting closer and I moved back to the B&B.Mr Black asked me to take a break from our jogging and spend a lot of time in his bedroom giggling with Mrs Black.I knew what the giggling meant.Life was good and Sandy asked me to drive to the ocean with her for a weekend before the commemoration event and I agreed.

The town people made sure everything was well planned and up to five star expectations.They even made sure the Rocksher farm was scraped and a solid slab of concrete was poured over it without a sign that it existed and they hired a whole lot of people to make sure it's done within a week.Pastor Shrouder decided that a tower with the names of all the heroes will be erected over the concrete slab over the Rocksher farm and it will become and official memorial site.A great idea to me.Its like telling the Rocksher demons that,"You tried to kill us but we are still on top of you."I am looking forward to my trip with Sandy. I can't wait to just be normal again.

I was coming out of the B&B when I saw a car speeding away from the gate.It was a silver Sedan with darkly tinted windows and I could see they were looking for someone or something here.I went it the house and told the Blacks what I saw and they all told me that they don't know a car like that or anyone that drives one.Who was that.I asked Sandy to take a trip with to the Night Owl because I bought a gift for my great aunt Yanda and it was just to apologize for not trusting her and all the love and support she gave me through this period.Yanda was a real pillar to me and she never gave up on me.Sandy decided to close Cuppa Jack for a week so we can prepare for our trip to the ocean.We took Sandy's car as my uncle Thomas was busy servicing my car for the trip.We passed by Cuppa Jack and Sandy checked if the refrigerators were fixed because she send one of her employees to take the technician to check the fridges that had issues.At Least they were sorted.As we drove away Sandy asked looking in the rearview mirror,"Bucket isn't that the car you saw this morning?"As I looked back I said,"Yes."Sandy turned around and followed the car and it sped off with a torque.We tried chasing behind but it was too fast, at least I managed to get the registration number.We turned around and went to Yanda at the Owl.Yanda was busy stocking up the fridges and told me us that many outsiders are coming to this town because someone leaked the story of our town and media houses wants a part of the action and some are even planning on writing movie scripts and books.So the Owl will be very busy.I gave Yanda her gift and she gave me a kiss on the chicks.Yanda offered us something to drink and I asked for some of her Peach wine I heard the Black's winery make fine wine and it's a sin that I haven't had a taste since I have been here and I even stay in their house without knowledge of how their wine taste.I asked for a whole bottle because I wanted the full experience.Sandy had some juice instead and she saw I didn't approve of her choice but she stuck to her decision and said,"One of us has to drive."We spent the whole day with aunt Yanda and she made us laugh with her childhood stories.She was a very sweet soul and she could hurt a fly.

The twins still stayed with uncle Stephen at the Brooks home and they were enjoying the winter out of summer.Horse riding and hunting trips and a lot of whiskey and meat.Sandy and I passed by on our way from the Owl and found the quartet, great uncle Stephen, Ricky, Johnny and uncle Paul.Uncle Thomas and Edmond's father Edgar Marx passed Sandy and I at the gate as we came in with Craig Shrouder riding in Thomas's car.The 4 were busy debating about which is better from a rifle and a machine gun.I didn't even want to answer when they asked about my opinion and my only opinion was," guns all kill the same." I called my uncle Paul to the side and gave him the registration numbers of the silver Sedan and he promised to check up on it.He is very good with machinery and IT stuff and I trusted him to get an answer for me.The twins told me they think of moving here and they love this town and the people.We went in the house, Sandy and I and we greeted my great aunt and told her that we are going to the ocean for a week and she wished us well.We said our goodbyes to everyone and left.At the B&B we asked Mr and Mrs Black if Maggie came back to fetch her stuff and they said no and she doesn't even answer their calls. I wonder where she disappeared to.I told Mrs Black that Sandy and I had a late lunch and I won't be coming downstairs for dinner. I am just gonna take a bath and get some rest.I took a long relaxing bath and it felt so refreshing.Back in my room I put on some music and lay down on the bed. Yes I wasn't afraid of strange beds anymore, this place turned me into a warrior now and I could face anything.I fell asleep on the bed with the music playing in the background when I got disturbed by a knock on my door.I opened and it was Sandy standing in front of me with this short see through night dress and her hair all hanging down to her shoulders.She had a bottle of wine and two glasses in her hand and said,"How about a night cap?" She looked amazing and my imagination was running a mockery on my mind.How come I never saw how beautiful Sandy was.With her red long locks.Irish blood I guess.Green eyes and little speckles on her nose that looked like someone painted them with a fine point marker.She smelled of vanilla and musk,must be her perfume or soap.She was walking barefoot.I looked over at the clock on my bed stand.It was 23h00."Sandy saw me look at my watch and before I could talk she kissed me and welcomed herself into my room.She pushed the door behind her with her foot and closed it.She put the wine and glasses on the dresser and pushed me onto the bed and said,"It's my birthday tomorrow and I want to celebrate with you starting now,into my birthday.And I am not gonna allow you to talk, because if I allow you a chance to say something you might just try and talk yourself out of this.So shhhh" She got on top of me as I lay on the bed and she has her way with me until the morning and we never got a chance to drink the wine.We fell asleep in the morning and she just lay there in my arms.I could see by the way she slept with a smile on her face that she felt happy and safe with me and I just held her.

Morning came and so did new things.Sandy asked me to join her for a morning bath and I didn't hesitate I might just get lucky twice, unfortunately I didn't get lucky this time because she wanted to take me somewhere today after we fetch my car and did our shopping for the trip.I was a little disappointed with not getting lucky a second time but I accepted that we have a busy day ahead and I will still get a lot of lucky days in my life with Sandy if the universe allows.At the breakfast table Mr and Mrs Black kept looking at us with smiles on their faces and I knew why.Sandy didn't waste time and kissed me In front of her parents and told them that we are gonna be out the whole day shopping for our trip to the ocean and they were so happy.We picked up my car from Paul and he told me that the registration numbers to the vehicle is registered to a Leonard Smith.I don't know any Smith but I asked him to do some more digging and find out if the car was reported stolen.

Sandy and I did our shopping and she took me to John's Eye.The place was on a hill and you could see the whole town from there.What a view.She told me that this place was considered holy ground and this is where the amulet of the Rocksher family was hidden and stolen.She told me how the first towns people used to come here and pray and worship before the church was built.Sandy was always so enthusiastic whenever she spoke about almost anything and made a simple topic like laundry sound so amazing that you would wanna do it all the time.We had a picnic and she told me about her ex and how he broke her heart by sleeping with her cousin.She told me about how as kid she and her friends would come here on the hill and play church.After hours on the hill and darkness approaching we packed up and went to see Paul again before going back to the B&B.Uncle Thomas could not find out who the Smiths are and the car wasn't reported stolen.As we left the Brooks house we saw the car again and it sped of again.

After dinner Sandy and I sat outside on the balcony and I remembered Zane Gold.Yes if Zane could track Thomas in Africa then he can help now.I called him and he sounded real chaffed to hear my voice.``Het Mr Brooks I heard what happened in Levensdown Parish.You guys are international rock stars now and all the attention is coming your way.Good and bad.So how are you Mr Rock star?"I just laughed and said,"You have real jokes hey Mr Gold?" He cackle with laughter.Hey Zane I have another story for you to investigate for me and I will pay this time.I will send you the details now.Please do it for me because I know you can?" He asked me what the details were that I will be sending him and I said," just look at your phone and let me know``.He agreed and told me that he doesn't want payment for it and feels like he owes me.The night was warm and winter was gone.The stars lit up the sky and the atmosphere was Sandy put her head on my chest and I looked down at her as she stared up into my eyes and we kissed passionately and I got caught in the moment and when my phone vibrated and rang and almost gave me a heart attack catching us off guard in the Sandy laughed and even threw herself down on the floor as she laughed at the way the phone startled us.It was Zane Gold and he didn't even take 15 minutes to get back to me.I looked at Sandy before answering and said,"Is this guy a magician or what.So fast?"He sounded even more excited this time.``Mr Brooks I got information for you.When you sent me the registration numbers and the names Leonard Smith.I did a cross reference check and the address that came up was 1290 Oval Crescent,Bingerville.And the only people I know from Bingerville is Maggie and her family.I got the contact numbers and called them.And to my suspension it was Maggie's brother Leonard who answered and he was happy to hear my voice because we knew each other from University days.He told me Maggie left her car at his house and borrowed the silver Sedan.Since it was just parked in the garage and nobody using it he borrowed Maggie because her car had issues to start."I asked myself one thing: why is Maggie hiding in the shadows and stalking me and Sandy?Zane also told me that Leonard told him that Maggie wasn't alone; she was there with her husband Michael.Why do I get a feeling things are still gonna get funky here?I told Sandy everything Zane told me and she said,"Sweetheart this has Karen written all over it."Sandy might be right but what if we accuse a wrong person and I mess up my new found family relationship with Karen without having enough prove.I need to find solid proof and I need someone they won't suspect as my spy? It's like everytime we move towards tomorrow, yesterday keeps coming back to haunt us.Will there never be rest for a soul like mine and what's so important and huge that I must remain the center of attention.If it was positive I would welcome it.But now it's only negative.I hope this trip with Sandy will bring some positive into my negative.But like my aunt Yanda always say,"Don't sleep nor slumber for the enemy awaits to strike."I won't sleep nor slumber.

Sandy and I lay up the whole night thinking about a spy and Sandy couldn't think of someone we could use and then I spoke to Ricky today and he told me that Frankie Dowde is the best man for the job.Karen knows Fred so that's out of the question,but she has never met Frankie because he wasn't even at my wedding day due to work related matters in Europe.Frankie should just come into town with the hustle and bustle that's gonna happen now with the press media and tourists coming into town and just blend in without being noticed.Ricky had a magnificent plan and it can easily work.Ricky promised that he will alert the Senate to work in the shadows and protect him.I know Frankie is sneaky almost like Karen and he can pull this off plus he has charms a lot of it.I told my great uncle Stephen about Maggie who is stalking me and I think Micheal is with her.Stephen told me that we should set a trap for them and find out where they hiding away in this town.Once we found out their whereabouts we need uncle Paul to put a tracker in the car so we can trace their movements.We called a

Aunt Yanda at the Owl and she told us that Kamily sleeps there but she hasn't seen Maggie or Micheal come there.The question is where are they hiding?

Uncle sent out the registration numbers to the Senate and asked some of the town people he trusted to look out for the silver Sedan.Thee days went by and still nothing.I think Maggie and Michael left town.Sandy and I decided that it time we leave for our trip to the ocean and they should keep us updated.Paul came to me and gave me a ring before we left and told me the ring belonged to my grandfather

William and he modified it by putting another tracking device into it and and he gave Sandy necklace with a tracker too just to know where we are all the time and should we move away from where we're supposed to be it show alerts that we might be in danger.Paul asked us to write a list of all the places we're going to visit to make it better to understand our movement and track us.We went back to the B&B and packed our bags into my car and said our goodbyes.We passed by the Owl and told my aunt Yanda and see told us that Kamily wasn't there she left early this morning.Sandy and I hit the road and it was a bit of a distance were we are going.We passed beautiful farms on the way and even saw some old heritage sites and an old museum.The scenery was amazing and my companion was absolutely wonderful and I enjoyed her company a lot.After 4 hours of driving we arrived at our destination.The hotel was next to the ocean and our windows faced the ocean.The view was breathtaking.It was Spring now,winter was gone and the weather is awesome.I could see kids playing on the beach and they enjoyed it just by looking at them.I helped Sandy unpack our bags and we went out to the beach.At the beach we just enjoyed a picnic and lay there watching the waves and people passing up and down.It was very refreshing and therapeutic for me and Sandy that just came from a horrible experience in Levensdown Parish.Sandy told me that she wanted to go back to our room when the security clears the beach later because she wanted to take in all this awesomeness at the beach and forget home and focus on us, and just chat and relax, that's what we did.

Days went by so fast.We went bungee jumping,Scuba diving.Shark snorkeling and even caught some big fish.We even went up on a mountain trail on a nearby island.Apparently the island was discovered by a slave who ran away from his master's and made a dingy and floated out here,he then built a boat and went back and fro stealing other slaves from his master's,he did that for years and the population grew until he was captured trying to rescue more slaves from the cruel masters.The master's tortured him to speak but he never did.There are 50 small islands in the area and they could know where o to go.The wicked slave owners ended up killing the slave because he never spoke.The island has inhabitants about 500 people and the house of the slave is as museum.The Island was discovered only about 10 years ago when a military helicopter flew over it and saw there were people down there.Since then people travel to the island as it became a tourist attraction.Sandy and I had an awesome time and we didn't have any hassles from Karen or anyone and nobody called us because I told them only emergency calls and nothing else.Sandy looked at me the other day and told me I have a glow.This proves one thing.Happiness.I am happy, after a long time.I felt alive again and Sandy made me happy.We had a day left on our trip and we decided to just spend it in our hotel room.We have done almost anything we can think of and it was awesome.Sandy and I made love and slept and woke up and ate and took a bath and made love again and did everything over again the whole day.Our time was up and our trip was over. We had a lot of fun and took tons of pictures of the trip for the family.We created memories of our own.Sandy and I.We hit the road back to the Yanda wasn't at the Owl we found Karen there and a lot of people even the media,we pushed cameras out of faces as we walked towards Karen.She pretended to look happy to see us.I could see in her fake smile and I knew her,after all I was married to this woman for years.She told us that Yanda went to see Mrs Black because they had finishing preparations for the commemoration coming up.As we were about to leave Karen stopped us and asked Sandy and I to sit down for a moment as she wanted to talk to us.We sat and she spoke."Bucket I just wanted to apologize for everything I put you through and hope you can forgive me.I was placed under a spell by our grandmother Clare because she wanted to use me as a weapon against the Brooks family and even from behind the grave she still has power over me.I almost destroyed your life and you are innocent.But rest assured it won't happen again and I will do anything in my power to protect you.You and Sandy have my blessings."I could see through her lies Sandy was up to away whispering in Sandy's ear,"Ok Kamily."Sandy only laughed when we got into my car.Maybe yesterday is gone and a new day is coming?

Chapter 18
I am Bucket Brooks

We found Aunt Yanda at the B&B and she and Mrs Black were busy packing boxes with trimmings and decorations.In the kitchen were five other ladies busy with menus. This proved that they want this to be a top class event and the press media will be here too.We greeted the ladies and Mrs Black said,"You guys look happy, why didn't you stay for another week?"Sandy told her that she would miss us too much if we did.We went upstairs to unpack our bags and just as I was about to be done a call from Ricky came through."Hey Pete, Frankie is in town but he will be staying at the Owl to see if Maggie comes around there.It wasn't a bad idea.He will just stay there as a guest and maybe create an alias like being a writer or journalist.I told Frankie to make sure Frankie doesn't make any contact with us because they might sniff something out.Another week went passed and one was left before the commemoration event and the town was a buzz.People going up and down.Reporters and tourists everywhere and shops and lodges filled.Some came with their own The Senate had a lead on where the silver and Sedan was and we had to send Frankie to check it out since they don't know him.Frankie had created fake credentials with the help of my uncle Paul.We even got him a rented vehicle that can't be traced back to him.Apparently Maggie and Michael his at a town next to the Gold mine owned by the Parish.The town was called Middleton.It was bigger than the Parish and many of the inhabitants of that town worked for the mine.Frankie was sent on his mission and given a hidden camera and a microphone that is concealed.

Frankie made his way to the address that he was given and to his greatest joy found the car parked outside.How stupid could these people be.If you're living a secret life keep everything secret.Its like hiding under a bed and your feet stick out from underneath the bed.Franklin knocked on the door and Maggie came to the door."Hey madam,my name is Joshua Bassett and I am a reporter from Yardersfield and I am here with other reporters writing stories on Levensdown Parish.We are also interviewing neighbors in nearby towns.Can I ask you a few questions?"Maggie welcomed him in.Frankie even spoke with a Irish accent and put on some spectacles and dyed his hair red.He was really in character.But that's how he is,all or nothing.Michael came out of the bathroom and asked,"Maggie who is at the door?"He came to the sitting room where Frankie was sitting and asked,"Who the hell are you?"Frankie got up and took out a business card.Michael didn't even want to look at the card and said,"I asked you who the hell you are."Maggie said,"Honey this is Mr Joshua Bassett, a reporter from Yardersfield."Michael got angry and said," I didn't bloody ask you to speak for your boyfriend Maggie."One thing that Michael didn't know is that Frankie did almost everything from boxing, kickboxing and taekwondo and could drop him with one blow. Michael started putting his hand on Frankie and pushed him around screaming,"Who the hell are you." Maggie came in between again and said,"Mr Basset please just go."Frankie threw a card on the coffee table and said,"Call me when you wanna talk."Frankie walked to his car and could hear Maggie screaming,"I am sorry Michael and it was clear he was beating her.Bloody bastard.Putting his hands on a woman.Frankie send us all the Intel proving it was Maggie and Michael and now we know where they are hiding.I could hear that Frankie was angry when he spoke to me on the phone,"You know Pete I wanted to walk back into that house and break that guy's neck."I told him that he shouldn't forget that this family doesn't fight fair.He would've probably used a spell or something on Frankie.Frankie did well not to fight.Maybe not now.

Ricky, Paul,Craig and Johnny went out to scout out the place Maggie and Michael stayed.It was late at night and Michael and Maggie were asleep.Paul and Ricky jumped into the yard while the other two put a tracking device underneath the car.Nobody even saw them.These guys are becoming natural Ninja's.Game On,now we will know where they travel to and track their movement.They went over to the Owl and put one underneath Karen's car too.Boys on a mission indeed.Johnny send me a message and told me about the tracking devices.A week went by and Maggie's car never came around Levensdown Parish and Karen's car also tracked inside the borders of Levensdown.The day was here for the commemoration and the town was even more overcrowded and swarming swarming with reporters and I believed that it was gonna get more wild as the news of Levensdown is spreading like wildfire and more people are to come.Pastor Shrouder will have to end up putting up a border gate to allow people to come in.The B&B was busy and swarming with men and women carrying boxes and plates and food around, loading them into vehicles and coming back again and again.It was crazy.Mrs Black was giving out orders and it's was only 5 o'clock in the morning.All this noise actually woke me up.Mrs Black looked over at me and said,"Go wake up Mr Black and Sandy and get down here to give a hand." Mrs Black wasn't the type you could say no to and I did what she said.Mr Black wasn't impressed with me and Sandy was just happy to get a morning kiss.By 9h00 o'clock in the morning everything was done and the town Hall was set up and tents at the Rocksher farm and outside the Dance Hall yard.The town looked amazing with decorations hanging from poles and trees and windows.Mrs Black told Sandy and I to go bath and get ready for the day is long ahead of us.I made sure that I enjoy wearing my tuxedo today.I got dressed and waited for Sandy downstairs.I hope everything goes well today because the last time the town gathered together at one place we faced a giant snake.What can go wrong today?

The Security was tightened this time around.I couldn't believe what the construction people did with the Rocksher farm.It was scraped completely and all the eyes could see was just concrete stretching far and wide.New plastic makeshift trees and grass was planted into blocks on the sidewalks and it looked clean.Benches and a huge stage was erected where the horse stables used to be and in the center where the house used to be was a huge concrete structure covered with a huge curtain.Ther were chairs placed all around to create more space for seating.Uncle Stephen was the MC and he got onto the stage and spoke."Ladies and Gentlemen I am happy to welcome you here today.We stand today on a place that was once the center of evil.This place was the cause of terror and death on this beautiful town of ours.Today we stand here and in remembrance of our fallen heroes.Today we are here to celebrate the heroes sitting here today.Today we celebrate the sacrifices by the people who gave everything for the greater good of those alive and to come.We stand on the place the place that took from us and we say.We are still here.We are still standing and still fighting. We are still on top of you.So Ladies and Gentlemen without further adieu I give you our Mayor and Pastor, Mr Shrouder.Pastor Shrouder walked onto the stage and said,"thank you Mr Brooks."Yes we are here to celebrate and remember our heroes.Those who willingly gave up their lives against a war with evil.People like Edmond Yeast and Gavin Right."Pastor Shrouder read the names of all the dead and then the living and I almost jumped up when he said Bucket Brooks , Sandy Black and he continued and said,"Let's unveil our monument."As he pointed at the huge structure.The curtain was lifted of and I saw the names of people on gold plates the crowd stood up and started clapping and screaming and the media took videos and pictures of Pastor Shrouder standing In Front of the monument.The music came on and people started dancing.Uncle Stephen came back on the microphone and said,"Ladies and Gentlemen we will be moving to the Dance Hall for further festivities and everyone is welcome."The drummer band led the way as we followed from behind.People danced and sang in the streets.Even Karen was dancing.The celebrating went on until the next morning at about 4 o'clock when Sandy,I,the twins, Frankie(who is supposed to undercover and I can't understand what he is doing here so late?), Craig Shrouder, the Blacks,Paul and his wife, Thomas and his wife and about 8 more other town people plus the DJ we danced and felt like we were 16 years old again.We left one by one until by 4h45 we had all gone home.Sandy slept in my room and we just talked and laughed and were so drunk that we just fell Yes with shoes still on our feet.

Still very hungover in the morning Frankie calls me and tells me he will send me some videos and recordings.Only thing that went through my mind was,"When did he record them because we came home this morning and it's only 6 hours ago."The messages came through on my phone and I couldn't believe it.When Frankie got to the Owl this morning at 5 o'clock he didn't see Karen's car in the driveway.A few minutes later he heard a car coming up to the house and he saw 3 people stepping out.Yes it was Karen, Michael and Maggie.Frankie took a video from his window as they came in,while hiding so they can't see he sat down and recorded from the corner of the window.Michael carried a small box that looked like a coffin but not bigger than 20 cm in length.They went up to Karen's room and Frankie went to the door and to record the conversation.He was drunk but still very stealth.I always told him that he was supposed to be in the army.He was a focused person, that's why he was the leader of the Blue Boys.He was almost caught but managed to run into a room next to Karen's room that was just evacuated.Luckily the door was standing open and he just went in and crawled under the bed.At Least the evidence he gathered was enough to hear what they were saying."Micheal spoke about the dagger of Jangala.And I could hear it was couriered from Africa.Karen got angry and said,"We need to find the amulet of Tomoko.Where did our grandmother hide it?"I forwarded the messages to the Senate to immediately.I send a message to Franklin and told him to make sure he leaves town and go back to Europe.Since Michael and Maggie come to the Owl they might identify him and he could be in danger.Frankie being Frankie, refused and told me he knows how to get information.He saw a loophole that he can use and it will give us a foot inside the hornet's nest.I couldn't argue with him because to be frank.Franklin always gets the job done.Frankie had a plan to charm Maggie and get her to sing like a cannery and she did.Frankie followed Michael tp see what and where he went and created a timesheet of Michael's movements.He knew when Micheal met with Karen and how many hours he would be away from Maggie.He knew when Micheal would follow me when I came out of the B&B and even when Michael walked on foot.Frankie monitored his every move and made his move too.Frankie went back to see Maggie again still under pretends of being a reporter.Frankie knew that Michael was abusive towards Maggie and beat her up.The bruises on her face that she tries to conceal with makeup is still evident.Maggie let Frankie in for the interview because she knew Michael would be away for some hours.Frankie could pick up on Maggie's tone that she was tired of this life and wanted a way out but she didn't know how.Frankie used it to his advantage and tola her he can get her into movies and television because she was very beautiful and he kept repeating how beautiful and intelligent she was and she really liked it,I mean really liked it.It was clear that Michael only looked at his wife as an object and nothing else.Franklin being slick as he is worked on her vulnerable side and boosted her ego until it hit the roof.She felt very comfortable talking to him and opened up about plans she has for her future.Weeks went by and they would meet whenever Michael was gone and the meetings started happening outside the house they rented.Frankie would take her for picnics and started romancing her as he could see she developed feelings for her and even if he doesn't want to admit,I think he developed feelings for her too.Almost a month went by and they started sleeping together and she started telling Frankie everything about Michael and his family.She told him about their history of sorcery and Karen.And then she told him how Karen hired her to follow me around for years now.Karen used Michael and Maggie to keep an eye on me incase Clare made contact with me.Karen promised them money and since Michael squandered all his inheritance due to gambling they were broke and Karen is their only way to a better life.She didn't enjoy doing it but she is scared of Michael and Karen and does what they say.Maggie told Frankie that they have a dagger called the Dagger of Jangala and Karen is in possession of it.They need the Amulet of Tomoko and with both Karen will have powers beyond control and she needs to find Clare too that's why they keep an eye on me.Frankie knew that he had to get Maggie some help because now that she has spoken her life if in danger.Frankie told Maggie that he had a wife but he didn't give her his real name and Maggie wasn't worried about him being married she just wanted to spend time with him and get him to help her get away from this life.Frankie reported back to us after a month with all this information and asked us to promise that we will help Maggie.

The Senate called a secret meeting and Frankie was put on video call because we didn't want him to be seen around us.Uncle Stephen asked Pastor Shrouder to explain what the dagger of Jangala is."Ladies and Gentlemen, the dagger of Jangala is a very rare artifact and there were only 3 made.Other daggers were made according to every Priesthood and they have different names, like the dagger of Babaze and Vougan.In total these daggers were 50 that was made and through history only one survived.The only one out of 3.The dagger of Jangala.Any Priesthood will kill to have this dagger because of its powers.The only thing that overpower this dagger is a amulet from a Priesthood were the dagger originate from.And in this case it's the amulet of Tomoko because the two artifacts originate from the same place.Now the dangerous part is if someone can possess both these artifacts they become the most powerful in the world.Now it is all coming together now.Karen didn't come here to help us.She came here to gain our trust thinking the amulet is hidden somewhere.She is more dangerous than the beasts we fought.What also made sense is how these demons obeyed her and feared her.She made slaying them so easy and now we all understand the motive behind her actions.Another thing is what they call the heart of innocence.In order to claim the power of the dagger and amulet combined,the person that has them both must kill and eat the heart of a blood relative who is directly related to the priest or Priestess who trained them.In this case it's you Bucket.Karem selected you long before you knew any of this.She is just waiting to find the amulet and then it's done with you.Now another thing that you have to know is the dagger is only used when the priest or Priestess that trained you is found and stabbed through the heart and their blood is drained and their blood used for bathing.So in simple terms is you find the dagger and amulet,kill the innocent relative and then your master."I listened to Pastor Shrouder lecturing us and then I put up my hand.I don't know why because I finished school long ago and this wasn't a classroom.``Pastor Shrouder.If you say kill your Priest or Priestess,then it means?" Pastor Shrouder smiled and said,"Yes your grandmother Clare is still alive."

Uncle Thomas said he saw his mother get burned on the stake and he buried her ashes.I had to turn to Thomas and ask,"Uncle who did you bury." He just shook his head with confusion in his eyes.``Johnny stepped forward and said,"Pastor, can I explain what happened here?" Pastor Shrouder agreed and sat down while Johnny spoke.``People there is a ritual in these wicked circles of sorcery called ukutwala.Its an African acronym for stealing the spirit of the living or dead,and to use it to anyway you want as long as you keep control over the spirit.With ukuthwala you can even zombify the living and dead and use them as clones to represent you when you're not even there.It's like shape shifting or out of body experience.With this ritual you can send your clone anywhere and people will think it's you.So when they killed Clare they didn't actually kill her but her Stunzela which is a African acronym for Shadow Zombie.So when burning a Stunzela you might not be killing the intended target.Well as a spirit person Karen knows it,but she doesn't know were Clare is and Clare is watching her from the shadows." Thomas spoke,"Now Johnny, if my mother is alive why doesn't she try to get these artifacts for herself and gain all the power?" Johnny looked at Pastor Shrouder and said,"Pastor over to you." Pastor Shrouder stood up again and said,"Clare is busy hiding from this evil about to rise and she looks in from the shadows waiting for the right time.I can guarantee that Clare saw Karen's motives when they got to Africa and faked her death.In this line of business if the understudy becomes stronger they devour the master.I sure Clare saw Karen's power rising and she has to run away from her until the timing is right.I believe that Clare is not far away and and she might be using Stunzela spells to hide in plain sight.I think Karen is using Micheal and Maggie to trail Bucket because she believes Clare will target Bucket or even try to warn Bucket.Either way she has to keep an eye on Bucket in order to trap Clare is she makes contact."

Stephen looked at us and said," Clare and might try to get Bucket under a spell and use him to get the amulet for her.Id she can have the amulet it will be easy to get the dagger because with the right spell she can trace the dagger but the dagger can't trace the amulet." I wasn't sure about one thing and I had to ask."Uncle Stephen,now if it's possible that Clare stole the amulet before she left town with uncle Thomas as a baby then why doesn't she just fetch it?"

"Well Bucket my boy,it is possible that where the dagger is hiding there is a group of different spirits hovering around it.The spirits are from both sides and there is war amongst them.And even if the spirits can see where the amulet is they don't have the power to take it because it will destroy them.They can only guard it from people trying to take it and anyone trying that will be devoured.Now I know you're asking yourself, why doesn't the spirits on Clare's side or on Karen's side just report to where the amulet is hiding.Well it's not that simple.The spirit world is sick and tired being controlled by the living and they will do anything to break that chain, so they won't help them.The only way to get the amulet is to use someone of pure blood and innocence to retrieve it from the hiding place.It can be a family member that has never practiced sorcery or a total stranger that bares the mark."What mark is my uncle talking about? " Ricky take out the scroll of Jangala,we need to check who amongst the Brooks family has the mark of Opal.The mark should be on the back of the left hand and it is shaped like a cross."None of us had the mark and I know 100% that Karen doesn't either.But who is this person with the mark and where do we find him/her.?

I asked uncle Stephen if I could just take a picture of that mark incase I see someone with that mark.He agreed but asked me not to speak around about it or I will endanger myself if I could speak to the wrong people.Franklin told me that he still wants to hang around and will only go back home if we have made sure Maggie ia taken care of and she is safe.After the risk he took and after Maggie put herself in danger I believe it is only fair to help her.The Senate sat down and discussed a way forward for Maggie and they agreed that we will have to create a new identity for her and help her financially so that she can start a new life somewhere else.Frankie made a few calls and used some of his family's companies to get Maggie a house and work in Europe about 400 km from where he stays just in case.The Senate set up her new passports and accounts and made sure we got her and Frankie away before Michael could realize she was gone.I would've loved to see the smile on Frankie's face when the plane took off and the anger on Michael's when he found Maggie gone.

Three days later after Frankie and Maggie left Levensdown Parish,he called me and told me he and Maggie arrived in Europe and everything went well.Maggie is living in a new home with a new identity and nobody will know who she is.He thanked me and told me to thank the Senate on their behalf.At Least some good is coming out of this bad.If these things never happened, poor Maggie would've died in misery and all this time I didn't even see her as a victim.Like the saying goes."Don't judge a book from the covers."

After speaking to Franklin I got up and took a shower and decided I should go for a jog.Sandy was out already and Bridget sent me a message saying she sent my daily report to Jones at work.I called Bridget and told her she doesn't need to do it anymore because I don't think I am going back there.She inspired me,Bridget.She just lost her husband and instead of mourning she still thinks about helping others.A heart of gold indeed.After my jog I need to pass by the library and see her.Mr Black wasn't in a mood for jogging nowadays and prefer the company of his wife more.I overheard him saying the other day that he must give Sandy and I more time together.He thinks that spending too much time with me won't allow our relationship to grow.As I passed through the graveyard I slowed down and saw as jogged towards the lake that some graves are dug up.The grave of William Brooks and another of Pascal Myburh.I already had an idea of why my grandfather's grave was dug up,but who is Pascal Myburh? I went to the Chapel to see if the caretaker was there.I knocked and no answer and I saw that the door wasn't locked.I walked inside and didn't find him.I went out and continued my jog around the lake and I looked over to where the Rocksher farm was and I could see someone standing next to the monument we unveiled for the town people and I could see he was really staring at it.As I looked closer I saw it was Michael but the car wasn't around.I think he came by foot or his it somewhere.He turned around a looked towards me and I stared back showing no fear at all.He didn't move and just stood there looking at me.I took the trail back through the graveyard and saw the caretaker.He was there with Pastor Shrouder and his son Craig.I ran up to them and told them who I just saw at the monument.The caretaker had a bandage around his head.And told us that last night while he was patrolling the ground.He saw someone busy digging up graves.He walked up to the person who has on black clothes and concealed his face.While facing the one digging up the grave another hit him over the head with a heavy object.He was lucky to be alive.We all knew who did this and kept quiet.I asked Pastor Shrouder who Pascal Myburh was and he told me that Pascal was the Pastor in charge of the church when the amulet was hidden so they thought that the amulet might be hidden in the graves of Clare's first and only love William or in the grave of the Pastor that had the Rockshers burned.It made sense that Michael and Karen will be looking here.I jogged back to the B&B and found Mr and Mrs Black in the garden doing whatever I just greeted them and went upstairs.I took a bath, changed clothes, grabbed my keys and phone and told them I am going to Cuppa Jack if they needed me.They just mumbled it under their chit chatting.They didn't even notice that I bumped over the trashcan in the driveway.Whatever it is they're doing is taking their attention away from everyone and everything.

I got to Cuppa Jack and found my sweetheart busy running up and down.The place was filled with faces new and old."Can I help with anything, Sandy?"She pointed to an empty table and said,"Just put your butt down I can manage."One of the waiters came over and asked "what will it be today Mr Brooks?"I was hungry from my jogging,but it was already 12 o'clock and too late for breakfast so I just ordered some chicken and chips with a beer.I looked over my shoulder when I said,"And a beer."Just in case Yanda was behind me.I could hear her say,"Drinking again Bucket?" She didn't want me to drink or maybe not excessively.I enjoyed my lunch and watched Sandy and her staff members going up and down.She came over to me and asked how my food was and I told her it was awesome.She kissed me and said,"Babe I won't be great company as you can see it's a madhouse here."I didn't mind just sitting there plus I would get some time to just think and familiarize myself with the faces.As I sat by the window I saw a lady standing across the street looking directly at me.I waved and she just turned around and walked away without waving back.A few minutes later a young boy stood at the same spot and looked at me the same way as the old lady did.I waved again and the boy waved back and called me outside by show of hand.I walked to the entrance/exit door and took my eyes of the boy for a split second and he vanished.I ran into the street and I couldn't see where he disappeared to.As I looked over my left shoulder I saw the silver sedan take the corner.But where did the sedan come from because I would have seen it take the boy,and it clicked.My grandmother Clare.The boy and old lady was Clare shape shifting.She saw the silver sedan driven by Michael and disappeared when I almost got close.The reality of the situation struck me now as I walked back to Cuppa Jack.I was almost or most probably abducted by Clare.Micheal is hiding,just waiting for me to identify Clare and then he will attack us both.He is letting me go because I am bait and nothing else.

I called Sandy over to my table and told her what had just happened and she got angry with me for being so careless.She told me to just remain here insight until she closed shop.She didn't want me to go outside alone now.I just think she wanted me next to her and this was a nice excuse.Funny.She sat with me at my table and ordered the staff to continue serving the patrons.We sat and chatted and ate and drank but my eyes kept wandering into the street.Hoping to catch a glimpse of Clare again.Time flew and we closed up, left Sandy's car at Cuppa Jack and took mine.The Blacks hadn't prepared dinner because they know that everytime Sandy and I spent together we don't eat at home.Mrs Black looked at us and said,"We are going to bed,if you guys are hungry you can make something to eat."We weren't hungry and decided to go to bed too.Sandy asked me to join her in her room tonight.Strangely I have never been in her room since I came here.Never.I went in and her room painted bright yellow and she had flowers painted on the ceiling and I didn't bother to ask about the decorations I just wanted to enjoy time with my babe and relax.

We fell asleep in each other's arms and it felt amazing.I went into a dream and in this dream I see my grandparents Clare and William sitting in my garden at my house in Firthlink.They are looking so happy and are singing while feeding each other grapes.In my dream I see my grandparents holding a silver jewelry bag and placing it in the ground.They then call me over and say,"Bucket you must keep this bag safe and never give it to anyone.Keep it safe until the marked one can bring it to the altar."I look over and see an altar with two stars on the front and a head of a bull on the top. Smoke rises from the altar and a voice screams from behind saying," bring the amulet?" In this dream my grandfather doesn't look at much and keeps looking at the person behind the altar and then he started bleeding from the eyes and ears and mouth.My grandmother started shouting."Bucket find the mark and the louder she shouted the louder the person behind the altar screamed at me.I couldn't see the person's face as it was covered by a mask with a dragon face.My grandparents started fading away but I could hear them shouting,"find the marked one." Sandy woke me up as I was screaming grandma in my sleep.I sat up and told her my dream.She said it clear that I must find the person with that mark on his hand and we need to find the amulet.But the one thing that is unclear is what to do with the amulet.I have one thing on my mind and that is to find this amulet and get the Senate to destroy it once and for all.Sandy told me to sleep and held me tight while putting my head on her chest and I fell asleep.It was 5:30 in the morning and Sandy was getting ready for her day at Cuppa Jack.I got up and told her I am going to my room to refresh and I will drive her to work. As soon as I stepped into my room my phone rang and it was Fred."Pete Mr Rogers woke up from the coma and they said he was looking for you.They couldn't contact you because only my numbers are on record at the hospital." I immediately called the twins and asked them to accompany me to Firthlink.We dropped Sandy at Cuppa Jack and went off.We found Mr Rogers sitting up straight and when we arrived at the hospital and he had a piece of chicken.I could see he was back to his old self.He loved his chicken.Mr Rogers only has a few bruises and bumps as if he was never in a accident."Bucket, Ricky, Johnny.I see the Blue Boys are back in town." We laughed at him and told him that we are happy to see him well again.He couldn't believe that he survived and came out of this coma and the doctors call it a miracle,but he calls it destiny."Bucket my boy you guys may think I am crazy with what I am about to tell you."And he took another piece of chicken before he spoke."Clare was here last night.I was still in a coma and had a dream.In the dream I saw myself going into the garden at the Rocksher mansion and saw Clare and William sitting in the garden eating grapes." I almost fell over and Johnny blocked me."Are you alright Pete?" Johnny asked while seating me down."I am not ok guys. I had the same dream about my grandparents sitting in the garden eating grapes." I told Mr Rogers my whole dream and he said,"Well Bucket my boy in my dream I didn't see the altar or the beasts behind the altar.I just saw your parents show me a hole in the ground with a silver jewelry bag and said give this to Bucket.Then I heard wake up Rogers and I woke up from my coma.And as I opened my eyes I saw Clare walk out of my room and I wasn't in a coma or sleeping.I really saw Clare last night."

This was mind blowing to me."Mr Rogers put his hand on my shoulder and said it's real Bucket my boy and what I saw next was even more mind blowing.The mark of Jangala on his left hand.He saw me looking at it and pulled his hand away.But it was too late.And by the time I wanted to grab his hand he said,"Ok I can explain.Lets go somewhere safe.Ricky took out the amulets we first used in our first battle at the farm when Edmond got killed, and said guys let's arm up we don't know what evilness lies near.We hanged them around our necks and Johnny said we should go to the school hall.There we can have some privacy.At the school Mr Rogers started speaking."Boys the Senate has been around for centuries and amongst us hiding and working in the shadows.The Senate has always protected us from evil. Normal regular people like doctors and teachers and even store owners.They go around unnoticed but are always around hiding in plain sight.No I am not part of the Senate but my family is and has been for centuries.Now within the Senate there has always been a chosen one that carried the mark of Jangala.Many chosen ones has helped the Senate destroy the dark ones,but many have used the mark to turn on the Senate and give power to the dark ones.Now the marked one is given the responsibility to be a guardian of the amulet and they are people that are pure hearted and innocent to the dealings of the darkness.And the ones that carry the mark don't form part of the daily dealings of the Senate and they have no knowledge of rituals and spells.They are just individuals chosen from birth to guard the amulet.The mark is the branded onto them by a spell to protect them from harm and the dark ones.So I was chosen as a infant and have been carrying the mark for all my life.My father who was part of the Senate told me about the mark when I turned 16 years old and told my about my responsibility and had me promise to secrecy that I would never speak to anyone about it and always conceal it by any means.I was lucky when Karen wanted to kill me she didn't see the mark on my hand.Now being the guardian doesn't mean you necessarily know where the amulet is hidden and it doesn't mean you have power to use it even if you have it in your possession.All you can do is guard it, retrieve it when needed and give it to the one that will use it positively to destroy evil.Sometimes a evil person can be the right one that you have to give the amulet to in order to destroy evil.As for me I don't know where the amulet is hidden.Now I know you're asking how Clare stole it from the farm before because she is wicked.The reason why she could take it is because the Dagger of Jangala was not around and anyone could take the amulet.But once a dagger is in the mix the two create a powerful force that only the guardian can withstand and retrieve from the hidden place.Once the dagger is around even if can be 20 states away the amulet can sense it and draw evil towards itself.The evil will hover around the hiding place of the amulet even if they can't retrieve it themselves and constantly fight against opposite sides and slaughter anyone trying to retrieve the amulet, accept for the guardian.The marked one can go in and out unnoticed by the evil forces."

I had to take a break away from where the twins and Mr Rogers where sitting.I walked to the window and looked outside.I could see the old jungle gym and the old swing where I broke a tooth.I just looked into the school yard and remember how easy life was back then.Our only struggle was Hurt and his goons.I stood there smiling enjoyed those few seconds standing at the window.And then I turned back to the group and my joy disappeared as reality hit me like a brick wall.Mr Rogers has to hide now,if Karen finds out he is alive she will come after him.Then my memory came back."Mr Rogers,do you remember sir that you said you saw Clare burying a vase in the garden of the Rocksher mansion at night?"Mr Rogers turned to me and grabbed me tight in his arms and said,"Brooks you biscuit.It makes sense now why there is evilness killing people at your house.The demonic forces are hovering around the amulet that is hidden there and they kill anyone coming in there.As a guardian with the mark they can't harm me and I can go in and retrieve it undetected."

I looked at Mr Rogers and the twins and said ,"I don't think it's the right time to retrieve the amulet. We need to know what Karen's next move is and how to destroy her and Clare both with one blow.Mr Rogers I think best solution is for you to hide in plain sight.You can't be harmed or detected by the demons and Clare or Karen won't go near because they can be devoured by the demons or the amulet.You will be safe at the Rocksher mansion." Mr Rogers and the twins looked at me and said,"your brain is working well today hey?" Mr Rogers agreed and now we have to consult the Senate on how to plan our strike.

We went back to Levensdown Parish and I called Sandy on the way to let her know I am fine and our trip was very fruitful.She told me that she will be closing Cuppa Jack a little late today as it's packed with more people coming into town.Many of the families in town are even providing their spare rooms and outbuildings as rentables for accommodation.Sandy told me to bring the twins around for dinner at Cuppa Jack.We got to the garage where Edmond worked to fill up on gasoline and my eyes just filled up with tears as I pictured the first time we met here and how he made my trip to the Parish sp easy.I can still see him standing at the at my car asking,"Where are you going to sir?"Edmond Yeast was a man that was gonna become part of my close friends.A man that I would invite to family gatherings.I miss him so much right now and tears are flowing from my eyes.Johnny saw me crying and put his hand on my shoulder and said "Edmond was a good man."The twins know that the garage belongs to Edgar Marx, Edmond's father and that Edmond and his brother worked here.One of the attendants filled my tank and we left.We passed the by the Owl and I went in to greet Yanda it has become habit to see her almost everyday and we have became close.As we walked into the Owl Karen came downstairs and saw me and the twins come through the door.She gave us this big snake smile and said,"hey cuz and twins."I didn't know what to say and just replied with a,"Hello cousin." She told us that she was going out to see a friend which was a lie.I had to play the fool just for fun and said,"Hey Karen when last did you speak to Maggie because I don't see her at the B&B anymore?" Her face turned red and she answered by saying,"I spoke to her just now as you guys came in and she is visiting a friend in Firthlink.She will be back by next weekend."I wanted to burst out laughing and stopped myself. Karen went out with her lies and I didn't even look at the direction she drove off into.I didn't care because I knew she was going to her sick demonic brother Michael.

Aunt Yanda wanted to offer us something to eat and we said no.We had s dinner date at Cuppa Jack with Sandy,but we had someone Peach wine and the twins even asked for a bottle each to take home.It was 18h00 and enough time for dinner when we left the Owl.As we drove into Cuppa Jack I looked down the street and saw the old lady waving at me and when I looked again she vanished.Dinner was 5 star and

Sandy even had a life band playing for the guests.Ricky called me and Johnny to stage and asked us to sing a song or two for the crowd.Sandy was surprised at how good we actually was.The crowd went wild.And we enjoyed playing again after years I asked Sandy to take a video we can send to Franklin and Fredrich.We wished all the Blue Boys could be here.Roars of encore rumbled around Cuppa Jack.We played 2 more songs before giving the band their stage back.Cuppa Jack was filled and we closed shop at 23h00 and went home.I borrowed the twins my car because we used my car the whole day and it would be a lot of up and downs for me and I have to drop them off so I gave them my car to use and Sandy and I used hers to get home.The Blacks were asleep when we got home and Sandy asked if I will be joining her tonight and I said I will be sleeping in my room tonight.She said,"Ok Brooks see you in the morning." I fell asleep and I heard something or someone coming into my room. I couldn't move I tried but I couldn't.I looked up and saw a dark shadow standing over my bed and it said,"They are coming for you beware Brooks."The shadow moved out of my room and I saw the door close and I could move again.I sat up straight.This wasn't a dream it was real and who was the shadow? I put on the amulet the Senate gave me and didn't sleep at all.Think I should move back to the Brooks house.I feel very exposed here.At Least until everything is done.

Next morning I called the Blacks and together and told them about my plans to move back to the Brooks home.I told them what happened and I feel very exposed.Sandy asked to go with me because she feared that Karen could come for her when I am not around.Mr and Mrs Black gave her permission to go with me.Uncle Stephen gave me and Sandy a room next to Paul's room and told me it belonged to my father Preston.The room was very neat and clearly showed that nobody slept there.At about 23:39 I heard the door of the room open again.I could see someone coming into the room.I whispered,"Sandy wake up,"and started shaking her but she didn't wake up.The person came into the light and it was Clare.She stood next to my bed and said," My grandson it's me.I am here to make things right don't be afraid.The beasts are coming but I will protect you."She touched my face and I could feel it was real it wasn't a dream.She was real.I got up and touched her hands and saw it was real.She looked up at me and said," I should have came back for you and your father but I was to busy looking for revenge.My revenge has put you in danger and I created a monster that is about to attack the world.I have seen this monster kill my love William and my son Preston and now it wants you my grandson.I fed this demon and I must destroy it."Tears started flowing from my eyes and Clare touched my face and said," Don't cry my beautiful grandson. I am here,"and she gave me a hug and I held her tight.I looked over at Sandy sleeping and my grandmother said,"She is beautiful don't worry your child will be fine." Clare told me that a great battle is coming and she needs me by her side.She gave me a amulet and told me to wear it all the time and I will be able to fend off demonic attacks from Karen and she gave me one for Sandy and told me Sandy was pregnant and this amulet will protect her and our unborn child.I said,"Grandmother I always needed you and wished to see you I would cry growing up and missed you."She hugged me and said,"I was always around.Bucket go to the Senate and show them the amulet I gave you.They know this amulet and they will tell you what to do.Please be careful and don't let Karen or anyone in this town see the amulet I gave you accept the Senate.Only the Senate must know about the amulet I have you and Sandy."Clare kissed me and said," go to sleep we will see each other soon my beautiful boy."She walked out of my room and disappeared.

The next morning I was still asleep when Sandy woke me up and said she wanted to go to the bathroom.I showed her the bathroom And stood outside I could hear her vomiting and I remembered Clare's word's last night.Sandy was pregnant.We took a bath and I took Sandy to the doctor.They made a test and told me Sandy is pregnant.I haven't told Sandy yet about my grandmother and wanted to speak to the Senate and the Blacks first we called Yanda and made sure Karen didn't know about our meeting.My father's twin Thomas was there also and I told them everything that my grandmother Clare told me.I told everyone that Sandy was pregnant and everyone was happy for us.I took out the amulets my grandmother gave me last night and uncle Thomas took out a scroll.She went to see him after seeing me and asked him to help in this quest.Pastor Shrouder took the amulets and said,"This one," holding up the yellow amulet," is for fertility and light.It is created to protect pregnant women and unborn children against the attacks of darkness and it is correct for Sandy and the baby and will protect them at all times.And this one is for battle against a power stronger than all and can only be worn by an innocent heart who is connected to the lineage of this amulet.A person with a pure heart and also the one needed for sacrifice." Pastor Shrouder saw me as I looked at him with widened eyes and said,"I know Bucket.You are want to ask why should you wear the amulet that will take you to the slaughter house.Yes you are the chosen one for sacrifice, but your grandmother has turned the tables around and given your uncle Thomas who is your blood line a scroll with a spell that will protect you.Now the one thing to get this done is to give yourself and your grandmother up as bait for us and Thomas to come through.It will be risky that's why your grandmother send you to us so that we can explain it to you.She knew you wouldn't trust her and think she wanted to trick you.So we need to make sure the tracking devices work that Paul gave you and so we can know where she's taken you.We also need need to tip of Mr Rogers to bring the amulet of Tomoko to where you will be kept in order for Karen to find.She won't know what's coming.She will just be happy that's as she has you and Clare and the amulet of Tomoko and the Dagger of Jangala."

Grandmother came to see me again this time she didn't hide from Sandy and told Sandy that she knows that we will be happy.She asked us to name the child William as she already knew it was gonna be a boy.Clare asked me to create an audience for her with the Senate to tell them what her plans where and I did.We sat up a meeting at the Brooks home and we made sure Karen didn't know and nobody in the town saw my grandmother.Sandy told her employees that she will be off a few days and they needed to cope on their own and report if they had issues and that was a request from grandmother that she rest.Every member of the Senate was available at the Brooks home including Mr Black who kept smiling at me.I could tell he was happy that I am gonna be his family officially this time.Yanda stood up and said,"Everyone welcome here and today is a day like no other for my brother's daughter Clare who we thought was dead is back to help us stop a greater evil that we have seen before.I know many of you here don't trust her.But I do and so does Bucket and Thomas.I ask you to just listen to her and decide.My grandmother who looked amazing for her age not much older from the pictures I saw.She stood up and spoke."Friends and family I know I am the last person you want on your side and the last person you trust but I understand.The Rocksher family has only brought death and evil to this town and towns away from here.I have been part of that evil for a long time and planned my revenge and build a following and even poisoning my own grandchildren Emily and Michael to become like the Rockshers so that I can pull out my plan for revenge.I am happy not all my offsprings fell into darkness and it showed that there was still good in my blood line.When Emily planned my destruction and I fled Africa I came here and moved into the shadows of Firthlink and lived in the Rocksher mansion.I was the one sending Bucket messages that said Brooks Tell Them What You Did.I wanted to instill fear in him so I can control him and then destroy him.But I saw how concerned and worried about Emily he was and took care of her even when she lied and kept secrets and brought demonic forces into his home.The day Emily was rushed to hospital I saw how he was falling apart and I knew that there is s still good left in my blood.The fact that Bucket looks so much like his grandfather brought back good memories and feelings about my only love William and I started loving again.I started protect my children for the shadows.I tried leaving messages for Micheal and Emily to change but they got worse just as what I saw in Africa that they are dangerous.Michael and Emily is beyond saving and their hearts are black.Not you Mr Black, sorry sir."Everyone laughed at grandmother's joke.

"And the two guys from the Senate Bruno and Glen was send by Emily and they pretended to be friends of Fred knowing very well they are double agents.Those guys were sent to sniff around for me and the amulet of Tomoko and they met me and I destroyed them.They were the only one I killed since I came back from Africa.Now I have a plan to allow Emily to capture me and Bucket and I want Thomas also to be captured to make the deal sweet for them.I want them to see me with Bucket and I want Bucket to move to the Owl where she will see us.I know at first she will pretend like she always does making it her mission to abduct us.We want her to abduct us and because you guys have given Bucket a tracker you will be able to track us.But you must make sure that you delay your attack because we want them to perform the ritual.Don't be afraid when I say I want them to perform the ritual.I saw Yanda and Mt Uncle Stephen smile and so did Mr Black.Well Stephen you need to get Rogers to make himself vulnerable to the Emily and her goons so they can force him to bring the amulet of Tomoko to them."Everything starts now so let's go.I took my bags and I took Clare to the Owl where we are supposed to stay.Same day Karen/ Emily/Kamily got us kidnapped and before midnight struck.We could not see where we were because of blind folds.Paul tracked the place via the trackers in my ring and watch.Karen took my ring and destroyed it and left the watch because it was a gift from her not knowing it had another tracking device.Thomas and Mr Rogers was send to the address to snoop around in order to get abducted by Karen's goons and it worked.Inside the old building that used to be a hospital for mentally ill patients grandma Clare and I were laid down on two altars for ritualistic sacrifice.We couldn't move because they strapped us down.

I heard footsteps walking towards grandma and I.There were alot of people around us chanting with black cloaks with hoods to cover their heads and faces.Someone came to me and took my blindfold of and said,"hi nephew."It was Isaac my father and Thomas's half-brother.And next to him was s big build dark man that took of my grandmother's hood and said,"hi Clare with and African eccent.Grandmother looked up and said,"You wicked man Bungari, you will burn in hell for this." He just laughed.Behind the main altar was my own wifey Karen.Dressed in a white Cloak with a black hood chanting strange words.Mr Rogers was summoned to bring the amulet of Tomoko forward to them and hand it to Mallam Bungari who was chanting something weird and foreign too.Karen was chanting something else and Mallam Bungari and the congregation was chanting something else.It proved that Karen was the leader. Mallam Bungari puts the amulet of Tomoko around Karen's neck and she starts chanting another weird spell and the building starts to shake a portal opens on the side of the main altar and demonic spirits starts coming through and bowing in front of Karen.Its clear Karen is to become Omni High Priestess and more demonic spirits comes through and bow In Front of Karen.Karen takes out the Dagger of Jangala and continues to chant but then Pastor Shrouder walks in and starts chanting something else.He is chanting the spell Thomas presented to the Senate.The demonic spirits stops bowing down and Mallam Bungari and Karen screams,"Stop you bloody fool."

Now this is what happened before we volunteered to be abducted.Clare set up a meeting with me and Thomas secretly because she believed there was a snake within the Senate and set a trap with a fake scroll that Thomas presented to the Senate.Clare also thought me and Thomas spells that we will use at the ritual house on her signal.This traitor had too much knowledge regarding the darkness and had answers for everything and Clare saw who it was and sat the trap.This snake within the Senate wanted to get the Dagger and Amulet for himself.So Clare knew that when she speaks about a delayed rescue from Karen,by the Senate ,the traitor will sneak away because he knows if he takes too long to get to the ritual house he will be too late to intercept the Omni ritual.Pastor Shrouder is standing face to face with Karen, Bungari and the congregation revving up demons with a fake spell.My grandmother wanted to send all her and our enemies to hell with one blow and she prepared the stage for this.Clare gave me and Thomas amulets of Battle called Kganya meaning the Light and ordered us to swallow them to conceal our motive.She did the same and when we got abducted they didn't find anything on us.Clare had given Rogers to plant the amulet of Wangera at the entrance of the ritual house to trap everyone including themselves inside.The Wangera amulet is to trap all living and dead in one space without escape when the amulet of Tomoko is activated.Mr Rogers was protected by the mark of the guardian he has and no force of darkness can harm him.Karen and Bungari doesn't know that the Dagger they exposed now is a fake one and Clare got Yanda and Paul to create a replica and put back into its case without her knowing.Like Yanda said,"Keep your enemies close."As Pastor Shrouder chants his fake interceptor spell that gets the demons angry, Karen and Bungari takes out a fake Dagger,the demons realize that the Dagger is fake and the amulet cannot combine with the fake Dagger, they turn on Karen, Bungari and the congregation.Clare orders Thomas and I to chat chanting the spell she taught us and as the 3 of us chant and Mr Rogers hiding under the altar I was laying on,the demon forces from the portal start pulling Karen, Bungari and the whole congregation into the portal to hell.Just as Clare wanted.The place is filled with screaming as all of them got swooped by demons into the portal.Clare looks at us as she gets dragged away and scream,Daddy, grandmother,Brooks please help me?" We all looked away until it was quiet.Clare ordered Mr Rogers to untie us and take the amulet of Tomoko away from here or we will be trapped in this place forever if the amulet of Tomoko is close to the amulet of Wangera.As soon as Mr Rogers took the amulet of Tomoko away from the building we managed to move out.We met the Senate coming in and told them Pastor Shrouder was inside sitting in a corner screaming, talking, crying and laughing at the same time.He instantly lost his mind and went insane when the demonic forces attacked.Sometimes in life you get what you wish for.He wished for crazy powers and he got crazy.

EPILOGUE

I couldn't believe Pastor Shrouder was a traitor.And nobody could.The Senate decided that Pastor Shrouder should be given a hero's death and die by his own hands.His name was removed from the monument and his family was put under what Clare called the witches test.To find out if they practiced sorcery,you get put under a spell without your knowledge and get tested to see what character comes forward.They all passed.The Rocksher mansion got cleansed and my grandmother and Mr Rogers lives there as a couple and she sees me every weekend.Uncle Thomas and his family moved back to the Parish.The twins got promoted within the Senate and travel world wide fighting evil and I became a full member.The Senate is always there so beware.Fred loves Europe and made it home.Frankie is still Frankie and takes care of his families,yes he has a child with Maggie.I want to visit them when William turns is a bit older.Yes Sandy is my wife now and Mr Black demand that I call him father.I do only when I need him to babysit William.We still jog and Bridget and her baby visit a lot.I bought the winery and I enjoy working there.Sandy still owns Cuppa Jack and became business partners with Yanda. Uncle Stephen is still the hunter and his wife joined him now and Paul and his family moved to the sea.Mr Creddle came out of his coma and moved out of Firthlink.Jones got to feel the hurt from Hurt and his wife divorced him for his non stop cheating.

The Senate is always watching and working from the shadows.You never know when you might need them or they might visit.It can be your neighbor or your teacher or even a family member.

My Name is Bucket Brooks.

Don't miss out!

Visit the website below and you can sign up to receive emails whenever Edward Bennie publishes a new book. There's no charge and no obligation.

https://books2read.com/r/B-A-ZOOAB-HQHOC

BOOKS 2 READ

Connecting independent readers to independent writers.

About the Author

I live to write and write to live.

www.ingramcontent.com/pod-product-compliance
Lightning Source LLC
Chambersburg PA
CBHW030648110726
47901CB00002B/622